There I Find Trust

Strawberry Sands Book Five

Jessie Gussman

Published By: Jessie Gussman

This is a work of fiction. Similarities to real people, places, or events are entirely coincidental. Copyright © 2023 by Jessie Gussman.

Written by Jessie Gussman.

All rights reserved.

No portion of this book may be reproduced in any form without written permission from the publisher or author, except as permitted by U.S. copyright law.

Contents

Acknowledgements	V
1. Chapter 1	1
2. Chapter 2	7
3. Chapter 3	11
4. Chapter 4	18
5. Chapter 5	27
6. Chapter 6	35
7. Chapter 7	38
8. Chapter 8	45
9. Chapter 9	48
10. Chapter 10	54
11. Chapter 11	60
12. Chapter 12	70
13. Chapter 13	73
14. Chapter 14	78
15. Chapter 15	83
16. Chapter 16	86
17. Chapter 17	93
18. Chapter 18	102
19. Chapter 19	105

20. Chapter 20	110
Epilogue	116
There I Find Hope	119
A Gift from Jessie	126

Acknowledgements

Cover art by Kim Killion of The Killion Group
Editing by Heather Hayden
Narration by Jay Dyess
Author Services by CE Author Assistant

Listen to the unabridged audio for FREE performed by Jay Dyess on the Say with Jay channel on YouTube. Get early access to all of Jay's recordings and listen to Jessie's books before they're available to the general public, plus get daily Bible readings by Jay and bonus scenes by becoming a Say with Jay channel member .

Chapter 1

"Congratulations on your new property." Michael Flanagan shook Griff Deant's hand. "I don't understand why you want to live up there in the middle of nowhere, but I'm happy for you, man. You deserve a little peace."

Griff grinned like he was supposed to and said some words of appreciation to his longtime friend and buddy.

They'd grown up together, Michael and he, although Griff had taken a few detours before he'd gotten to where Michael had gone straight as an arrow.

After he'd gotten there, Griff had realized that the white-collar life wasn't for him.

That didn't keep him from working hard, and most people would say he had gotten lucky.

He would have said that God smiled on him.

Regardless, he'd gotten himself out of the rat race as quickly as he could, although he hadn't planned on settling down in Strawberry Sands.

"I've never owned a beach house before. So it's a first."

"I think that's the thing with successful lawyers in Chicago. We all have beach houses."

"Well, I'm no longer a successful lawyer in Chicago, so maybe I'm a little late to the party, but I got here."

"Being late to the party seems to be the story of your life. I've never seen anyone take so much garbage and turn it into gold the way you have. Usually drug addiction sinks a man faster than a stone." Michael shook his head, slapped Griff on the back, and they exited the big conference room together. It wasn't like they needed all that area. There had been stacks and reams of paper to sign, but it'd only been Flanagan and himself in the room.

What would Chi say?

He found himself asking that question in his mind over and over again since he started working at her diner several years ago.

He didn't know why, since Chi didn't seem to give a flip what he thought, even though he couldn't seem to get her out of his mind. It was the first time in his life where he truly understood the meaning of unrequited love. Unfortunately, most of the town of Strawberry Sands knew exactly how he felt. Even worse, they knew exactly how Chi felt.

At least it was a small town.

"How about lunch?" Michael said as they walked to the reception area together.

"I'll pass. I've got a couple-hour drive up to Strawberry Sands yet, and now that I have the key to my property, I think I'd like to get settled in. We've got that winter storm coming."

Michael slapped him on the back once more, understanding that it wasn't a personal thing for him to turn the dinner invitation down.

Griff had always done better by himself anyway. Because of the things he'd experienced, he just wasn't like everyone else. Strawberry Sands suited him much better than Chicago. Maybe even being a short-order cook matched his personality better than being a corporate lawyer.

None of it was very satisfying. Possibly because there was still something in his soul that just wasn't filled.

Not that Jesus wasn't enough. He was. There was just...a disquiet he couldn't seem to shake.

Maybe that was the way everyone felt and no one ever talked about it.

He considered that on his way north toward his new hometown.

He'd been living in an apartment over the diner since he arrived in Strawberry Sands, and he was content there. But it wasn't every day that a man had the opportunity to purchase a beach house a ten-minute walk from where he worked.

The only thing that kept Griff from jumping on it to begin with was the fact that he didn't want to purchase it alone. He wanted Chi beside him. And if she didn't like it, they'd look until they found one that she did.

The one he just purchased was a little pretentious, definitely bigger than he would ever need as a single man. But he could dream. Maybe it would be filled up with children at some point. And a wife. He definitely wanted a wife. Although not just anyone. Maybe some men could go around and find any pretty face that would do, but he wasn't really interested in pretty faces. He...could only seem to get himself interested in Chi.

Of course, the second property he'd just bought held a lot more hope that Chi would be excited about it.

In fact, he could barely wait to tell her about it.

Maybe he drove just a little faster than he should have on his way north, because of the excitement of that second property. It was much less expensive than the first, much smaller, and not nearly as nice, but it was the one he knew would make Chi smile.

He wasn't sure when it happened, when making Chi smile had become one of his focuses in life. In fact, perhaps the main focus, other than making food for the diner. Especially strawberry recipes. Of course, the bottom line with that was making Chi smile as well. After all, if his strawberry recipes brought people into the diner, that definitely made Chi happy.

It was almost too cold for him to ride his bike, but the leather kept most of the chill out as he pulled off the interstate and took a two-lane toward the beach.

He hadn't told Chi what he was doing, just that he would be late for work this morning. He was never late, and he never missed; this was only the second time in the years he'd been working for her that he hadn't been there if the diner was open.

Even snow didn't keep him away, considering his apartment was just above the diner.

As he motored into town, he noticed there seemed to be more people than usual at the diner.

That wasn't necessarily a good thing. He didn't like taking a morning off and having the place get busier. That didn't say a lot for his popularity.

But he wasn't worried. He knew the food he made was good. He knew the recipes he made were popular, and he knew they helped make a place for him in Strawberry Sands, enabled him to give back to the community and to try to make up for the beginning of his life which had been a lot more take than give.

He'd made up everything that he needed to yesterday in order to have the special be easy for Chi to put together on this chilly, early December day, with dark gray clouds overhead and water that reflected the sky's mood.

He loved how Lake Michigan changed with the weather and the seasons and with a mind of its own.

He'd been fascinated with the lake since he first saw it, and while the house he bought might be a little ostentatious, he finally closed on a place where he could look out from almost any window in his house and see what she was doing at that very moment.

He parked his bike along the sidewalk, chilled to the bone.

He wasn't used to driving the whole way to Chicago, and if he made a habit of it, he'd have to get a regular vehicle.

Michigan was not suited for motorcycles from about October to April. Thankfully they were in the middle of an unseasonably warm spell which was supposed to usher in a huge snowstorm along with a massive swing downward in temps.

Still, he was partial to his old roadster and normally did not spend a lot of money.

It took a bit to get in the door of the diner, talking to the patrons and chatting about the weather, town life, and pretty much anything. Everyone was familiar, and everyone was a friend.

It felt odd though, like there was something going on that he couldn't quite put his finger on. Like people were holding something back from him. It was a strange sensation, but he felt like that more than once when people stopped talking midsentence and then changed the subject quickly.

Normally just as they were talking about Chi. Odd.

He made his way to the counter, then stepped behind and walked to the back. He saw Chi take a load of dishes back, and he figured he'd stick his apron on and start cooking as soon as he washed his hands. But he really wanted to share his news with her. This seemed like a good day to share it with the community as well, since there were so many people in the dining area, and it wasn't even lunchtime.

"Hey there," he said as he stepped in. Chi's back was to him as she moved the dishes off her tray and onto the counter by the sink.

"You're back. That's great." She barely smiled at him as she turned around, grabbing her tray.

"I am." He kind of wanted to tell her at a special time. To have the two of them together, talking, so he could surprise her with his good news, but the way she seemed so distracted, like she didn't even care whether he'd come back or not, bothered him, and maybe he wanted her attention, which was why the words slipped out without any type of fanfare.

"I bought the piece of property at the end of the street. The one where we talked about moving the diner. Where patrons can go out on the patio and eat with the great views of Lake Michigan."

That was a lot more than he normally said. He'd learned from a young age to keep his mouth shut and his eyes open. But he rambled just a bit, because his words didn't even make Chi stop moving. She had been throwing the garbage away, scraping off plates, and checking the food on the stove.

As soon as he was done, she spoke, not even looking at him.

"I told everyone today, and you might as well know too. I'm closing the diner."

Griff knew he was supposed to say something. This was a conversation and was his turn to talk. But his mouth wouldn't move. It had fallen open, and he couldn't close it.

Chi grabbed the rag along with the pan of water, shoving her tray under her arm, and began to walk past him.

"You're closing the diner?"

He'd just bought property. Planned to stay. To help her move the diner where they'd talked about.

"You mean you're closing it in order for us to move?" It was a question, but he tried to say it like a statement. Like he knew what she was talking about.

"No. Like I'm closing it down and moving to Chicago. The lawyer that I've been seeing has invited me to move in with him, and I've accepted."

He blinked. Then blinked again, his mouth still feeling frozen in an "O" position.

She was going to move in with the dude?

That wasn't Chi. She wasn't like that. Of course, he knew that was typical. People did it all the time, but Chi was different. She had morals and values and standards, and she tried to live by them.

"When?"

"Today's my last day." She spoke simply, like she didn't just explode his world with the other statement she made, and that she hadn't totally taken his job. Usually there was at least a two-week notice.

Although, he knew there were times where owners just didn't show up for work anymore, and a closed sign in the evening ended up being permanent.

But he never thought that would happen here.

"I was going to offer to sell this to you, but I guess if you've already bought the property at the end of the street, you won't want this one. I'll be putting it up for sale, so make sure you get any personal items out at the end of the day."

Right. His personal items.

What about his heart? She didn't understand that it was right here in the kitchen with them, in her possession. When she walked out, moving in with her high-dollar, fancy lawyer from Chicago, she'd be taking it with her. He wished he could stop her, but that wasn't exactly something he had control over.

"Actually, if things slow down this afternoon, I'll be closing early. So just wanted to let you know," she said, and then she breezed out of the kitchen.

Griff stood silent, his chest heaving up and down. She was leaving. Closing the diner. Moving in with another man.

That was the thing.

Closing the diner, he could handle. He didn't need this job.

Leaving might be a little harder, but if she were leaving to open a diner somewhere else or even get a job somewhere else, he could handle that as well.

But moving in with another man? And that slimy, big-city lawyer, who was a crook and a cheat if Griff had ever seen one. And he'd seen plenty.

But he couldn't tell that to Chi. She wouldn't listen. She wasn't interested in his opinion on who she dated or…apparently who she moved in with.

He swallowed, wondering if there was any point in even walking over to the stove and getting started at the job he loved.

He loved it because of Chi. Although, he definitely found a solace and a certain type of relaxation and contentment in cooking. In feeding people. In making things that they loved and ate and enjoyed. Making people smile, but most of all Chi.

Griff stood staring at the door, discouraged and heartsick where he had spent the last few hours excited about the news he had, and now that it had been a letdown, he looked over where he'd stood for so many hours at the stove, working, because he enjoyed it, true, but mostly because of Chi.

He had one day left, but it didn't matter. If she hadn't noticed him all the other days that he'd been there, today wasn't going to be any different. Why stay?

Because that's what a man of character did.

Chapter 2

Chi carried the tub of water out so she could scrub off some tables.

The diner had been dead that morning without Griff. He was the lifeblood. She, like everyone else, just orbited around him.

But she'd been thinking for two weeks about the proposition that James had made to her. He said because of his commitments in Chicago he couldn't come to Strawberry Sands and date her, but he could move her into his penthouse in Chicago and they could live together. He'd insinuated that if it worked out, he would be asking her to marry him. The way he said it made it sound like it would be a very short time.

She hadn't wanted to do it. That wasn't the way she wanted to live her life. But she wanted the respectability of being with someone who was successful, rich, suave, and sophisticated.

Right now, as the owner of this dinky little diner, she was barely any better than she had been five years ago when she'd been down and out in every sense of the word.

She'd determined at that point, maybe a little like Scarlett O'Hara, that she would never be looked down on again. People would not stick up their noses as they walked by her, acting like they were so much better than she was. She had determined that she would be successful no matter what she had to do. Success being defined by money and prestige and position in society.

James had it all, and she intended to have it all as well. As his wife, on his arm, she would be in the upper echelon of Chicago society.

She wouldn't have to worry about money again, and she wouldn't have to be self-conscious about how tiny her diner was and how small her salary.

Sure, she would miss the small-town atmosphere and the friends that she'd made here.

She'd miss Griff most of all. But she wouldn't allow herself to feel sad about that. Griff was self-sufficient. And he'd already bought the property that they'd been talking about purchasing for a while now. He'd done it without talking to her about it and telling her that he was going to. She wanted to turn on him, yell at him, ask him how he could do that to her. It was her diner. She should have been the one to purchase the property.

Of course, it had been for sale for a long time, and she hadn't made a single move on it, so she could hardly get upset, but still. That was her property. And Griff knew it.

Not that it mattered, because she'd already decided that she was going to move to Chicago.

Once word got around about that, people had started showing up at the diner just to see if it were true.

It was a good thing that Griff had made so much extra food ahead. If he hadn't had the foresight to do that, she would have run out of food. She could cook, but she couldn't waitress and cook and bus tables at the same time. Plus, people wanted to talk today.

Thankfully, those people weren't super eager for their food, since they came more for the gossip than out of hunger.

The only problem was, she had a nagging feeling that there was something that was just not quite on the up and up with James.

"I'm so excited for your new move," Kristin said, smiling at Chi as her girls looked over the menu.

"I'm excited too. I've always dreamed of living in the big city, and this is my chance," she said, finding that as the morning had worn on, she had to make more and more effort to infuse excitement into her voice.

When she had been face-to-face with Griff, she had almost chickened out and decided that she didn't want to move after all. Avoiding his eyes was the only way that she was able to tell him without bursting into tears and begging him to... She didn't even know what she wanted him to do, just knew instinctively that he could fix everything for her. She wanted to fall into his arms. Except Griff didn't look at her like that. He looked at her the same way most people did, like she was a roach underneath his shoe.

Never mind that Griff was probably from the exact same background that she was. Maybe not with the Amish Mennonite roots, but he was just as familiar as she was with the bar scene and all the things that went with it.

"We're going to miss you so much. The diner has become such a huge part of Strawberry Sands. And Griff, oh my goodness. And all of the strawberry creations? I just feel like crying. Even while I'm so happy for you."

See? That was what she meant. Griff overshadowed everything. He was so good at what he did. Whatever he touched seemed to turn to gold. People loved it. Especially the ladies of the town; they swooned all over him.

He wasn't even the kind of man that most small-town girls would be interested in. He was completely bald, with two hoop earrings in one ear, tattoos, of course the bulging biceps were a huge plus.

He must have nothing but weights upstairs in his apartment, although she'd never seen him moving any in. Maybe he just spent the evenings after he cleaned the kitchen doing push-ups or something.

Regardless, with his signature work boots, worn blue jeans, and tight T-shirt... He was the stuff of any girl's dream.

Hers included, except she didn't want to like him. Not like that. And she'd made a concentrated effort to only see him as an employee.

She wanted to like someone in a suit and tie with shiny shoes and a briefcase in one hand and his cell phone in the other. Someone who had a house in the suburbs or a penthouse downtown.

Someone like James.

He didn't exactly make her heart beat fast, not like Griff could.

She didn't even really enjoy talking to James, because he spent a lot of time complaining. Complaining about the commute, his workload, his partners at the law firm, or the weather.

She didn't mind listening to him tell her how none of the other women that he'd ever known matched up to her.

She liked that kind of complaining.

But she hung on his every word, laughing at all of his jokes, even the ones she didn't think were funny, which was most of them. She had to admit she didn't even get some of them. But she laughed anyway, admired him, and fussed over him any time he set foot in the diner. Just because he showed a little interest in her, and she saw him as her ticket out.

Although, less and less she felt like getting out.

There was a part of her that was sad at the idea of leaving Strawberry Sands.

There was a bigger part of her that was sad that he wanted her to move in and hadn't offered her a ring. Or any kind of commitment.

She moved around the diner, smiling at her friends, pushing aside the thoughts that she was going to miss these people. These people who had rallied around her, supported her when she was down, and loved and encouraged each other.

She was moving on to a new part of her life, and she was going to look forward to it. She was not going to look back with any regrets.

If only that nagging sensation that there was something that was not quite right with James would leave her alone.

Chapter 3

Griff wiped his skillet out for the last time, loving the way the cast iron glistened under his rag. He'd seasoned it, which he did every evening after he was done using it all day, and placed it on the hook above the stove.

Who knew who was going to buy this place, but when they did, the skillet would be there, ready for them to use. It was a good one.

Silly that he was thinking about a skillet like that, when the woman he really was going to miss was moving around behind him.

They closed down together every night. They opened together every morning. They'd been doing it for several years.

He had hopes that someday they would go home together, raise a family together, watch sunrises and sunsets together.

None of that was going to happen.

But he couldn't get the idea that he wanted to warn her out of his head. James was not what he seemed.

He didn't know if he could get the words out. He knew he didn't take very well to people warning him. Especially when he had decided what direction he was going to take, and he was ready to walk down that path. He didn't want people who had ulterior motives trying to "help" him by telling him not to do what he was doing. Especially when they had so much to lose from his decision.

If he were Chi, listening to her hired help tell her that she shouldn't close the diner down...he'd roll his eyes and think of course they didn't want him to shut it down. After all, they were losing a job.

Still, he considered Chi his friend, even if she was never going to be more.

"Are you leaving tonight?" he asked as he stood at the stove, staring at the back wall, not turning around to look at her.

Something moved, the swish of a cloth on the counter.

"Yes. As soon as we close up."

"Are you sure about this?"

"Are you questioning me?" she asked, and there was a warning note in her voice.

"You're an adult." That wasn't really an answer, but the honest answer was yes, yes, he was. He was questioning her. He thought she was about to make one of the stupidest decisions of her life.

"Then just wish me good luck. It's that simple, Griff. You don't have to be angry about it."

"I'm not angry." He looked over his shoulder, surprised that she would say that he was angry. Upset, heartbroken, torn up, desperate to keep her, all of those accusations would be true. Angry? No.

Anger never solved any problems for him, and he hardly thought it was going to start now. There was no point in being angry.

"You acted angry all day. You barely spoke to me. You barely spoke to anyone. And you burnt something. I can't remember you burning anything in the entire time we've had the restaurant open. How do you burn soup?" She shook her head, like she couldn't believe it, and then continued to wipe the counter that she'd been wiping for the last five minutes.

She was more upset than she wanted to let on. Was that because of him, or was it because she really didn't want to go?

He turned around, leaning against the stove and crossing his arms over his chest. He put one booted foot over the other and narrowed his eyes at her.

Business had died off, and it was only four o'clock, but they were closed. Dusk had fallen, made even more dim by the low clouds that still gathered over the lake.

"I think you're making a mistake." There. He said it. He could warn her. Even though he knew it would make her angry in her current state, and he couldn't think of any way to say it that wouldn't upset her.

"Really? That's interesting. Perhaps you think I'm making a mistake because you're losing your job."

"Yeah," he said, moving his eyes away from hers and looking at the far wall without seeing it. It's like she had forgotten that he had bought the property at the end of the street. He had a diner. All he had to do was open it and hire a waitress. It wouldn't be the same, it would never be the same, but he could be up and running in a month. After Christmas.

"Spit it out, Griff. What's the issue?" She stopped what she was doing, planting her feet and crossing her arms over her chest, her very posture screaming that she was challenging him.

He didn't want a challenge. He didn't want to fight.

"Living together, Chi? Really?" He hesitated, and then he said, "If he's a man of character, he'll give you a ring."

Yeah, that hit her where it hurt. But there was no pain in her eyes. The annoyance that had simmered there burst into full-fledged fury.

"How dare you judge me. That is ridiculous. You're going to go around here all high and holy telling me how I'm not living my life right? How dare you judge me?"

"I'm not judging. You can look at me and see that I've obviously made mistakes. Done things I regret. I've screwed up, not just my life, but the lives of other people. I was just...trying to help."

"You're trying to help by telling me that it's immoral to live with someone? Maybe those values are old-fashioned and outdated, and you need to get with the program. Everybody does this."

"Everybody?" He had so many other things he wanted to say, but it seemed like she was determined to think that he was judging her rather than trying to help. And there wasn't too much he could do to convince her otherwise.

"You're splitting hairs. Even Christians know that premarital sex is not a sin, and living together is a good idea. You find out whether you're compatible with someone or not, and you have less chance of divorce."

That wasn't the slightest bit true, and he could give her verse after verse to disprove what she just said, but he didn't need to. She knew it.

"If you're afraid of commitment, you're probably not going to have less chance of divorce. I'm pretty sure if you look up the statistics, you'll find that people who live together are more likely to get divorced. It's because they don't have the guts to make the commitment to begin with."

He probably shouldn't have phrased it like that, but he was annoyed at that slimy lawyer. If he wanted Chi, he could treat her like a lady and not like she wasn't worth anything.

But that really was judging, and while Griff felt like the man deserved a little judgment, because he wasn't giving Chi what she deserved, and he was pretty sure the man was already married, it would only make Chi more angry at him.

It would give her something to fight with him over and bond her to James. He wasn't going to divide and conquer there. Chi was loyal if nothing else.

"I think you're making that up. After all, common sense says that you live with somebody and you figure them out. You decide whether or not you're compatible. Regardless, you're not going to change my mind."

"I know. I'm sorry." He wasn't quite sure what he was apologizing for. Making her angry, he supposed. When he first started, they hadn't fought. But since James had come, he felt like she had slipped away. The gulf between them was probably his fault. He'd allowed it to stretch there, because he couldn't stand to see her with someone else.

She narrowed her eyes in suspicion, like she wasn't sure what he was apologizing for either.

"I don't want to fight. I don't want that to be our last memories. I've... I've enjoyed my time working with you, and I'm sorry to see you go. I wish you the best." The very, very best. He supposed that's what love did. Even though he didn't agree with what she was doing, even though he wished that she had chosen him, even though his heart was breaking, he wanted her happiness above all.

"I hope things go well with you too," she said, then she turned away like she didn't want to talk about it anymore. "If there's anything in here that's yours, you can grab it on your way out."

"I took a bunch of stuff out earlier." He almost told her he bought a house. But he didn't. "Do I need to move out of the apartment? You didn't mention that earlier."

"I'm going to be selling the place. You probably should. Who knows what the new owner is going to want to do with it."

"Yeah. Who knows."

He curled his fingers into fists, then shoved his hands in his pockets. He wanted to grab her, shake her, get some sense into her head, or maybe kiss her senseless. Yeah, that last, that's what he really wanted to do. But there was certainly no way that was going to happen. He wasn't going to force a kiss on her that she didn't want. That wasn't what he wanted. It wouldn't be any fun if he was kissing Chi, and he was the only one enjoying it.

He hated that they were parting on a sour note, but he didn't know what to do to fix it. He couldn't tell her she was making a good decision, and he'd already wished her well. He wasn't going to let her know how he felt, there was no point. She'd already made her decision, and it wasn't him.

Anything he said along those lines would sound the same as anything he said along the lines of not wanting her to go. It was just for his own selfish gain.

He didn't want to be selfish. Especially when it came to Chi. He wanted to do whatever was best for her.

"I guess maybe I'll see you around. Maybe I won't," he said, and he didn't really wait for her to say anything else before he walked to the back door and stepped out.

A lot of times in the evening when he got done early, the kid that he had been mentoring, if a person could slap their informal conversations with such a label, would be hanging around, and they'd walk to the beach, chatting or maybe just standing in silence.

But he didn't see Rodney standing anywhere, didn't see the black coat that he'd taken to wearing, the Gothic look that seemed to be cool but was just an open door into a spirit world that most people didn't understand.

Griff himself didn't understand it. He just knew that the Bible clearly said not to give place to the devil. That there was a spiritual warfare going on, and that even the Archangel Michael, one of the most powerful beings in the created world, would not contest with the devil but instead had the Lord rebuke Satan.

If the Archangel didn't want to mess with Satan, Griff figured that any human was foolish to open up their heart and mind to such a thing.

"Hey," a voice called from between two buildings as Griff walked down the sidewalk toward the lake. He had his hands shoved in his pockets although it was still unseasonably warm.

"Rodney. Didn't see you there." He spoke casually, trying not to show that he was relieved to see him. He worried about Rodney.

Rodney hadn't said exactly what was wrong, other than there were issues with his parents. He came from a wealthy family, his dad worked in Chicago, and the family made their main residence at their beach house near Blueberry Beach.

But Rodney hung out in Strawberry Sands. Griff hadn't figured out quite what had set him off, but he'd gone from being a fairly normal kid to one who slunk around, wearing black and playing fast and loose with the spirit world.

"Yeah, I was talking to a friend. I wasn't sure whether you'd be out tonight or not. Seemed like the diner was pretty busy."

"It is. Was. It's the last day that it will be open, since Chi is moving to Chicago."

"She's really shutting it down?" Rodney asked, falling into step beside him as they continued walking toward the beach.

"Says she is." A gust of wind blew, and Griff shoved his hands even further in his pockets.

Rodney twirled his coat around him, pulling it tight, even though the temperature really didn't call for a coat.

"How was school?" Griff asked, holding his breath. Rodney had talked about quitting.

"Same old crap. Different day."

"Where do you see yourself in five years?" Griff asked, knowing at that age he hadn't seen himself anywhere. He'd been very much like Rodney. Very much into anything that was dangerous, dark, daring. He flirted with alcohol and drugs and hung around other people who did the same. He'd been lucky, or maybe he should say God protected him. A lot of people he knew died young.

"Somewhere far away from here," Rodney said, sounding bitter.

"Do your parents know that?"

"No." Rodney laughed with derision. "If they did, they wouldn't care."

"Are you sure about that?"

"Yeah." Rodney snorted. They'd reached the sand, and they turned north without saying anything. "Dad's too busy with his mistress. I think my mom is having an affair too."

Ah. That explained a lot. It was the first time Rodney had shared what was going on at home. It made sense, but it complicated things too. Griff couldn't help to put his family back together.

"You know, parents aren't perfect. We like to think that they are, but they're human just like we are."

"My parents don't even try. They're too busy looking out for themselves."

Rodney probably hit it on the head. Marriage counselors might say that money was one of the things that caused the majority of divorces, but it was just a matter of selfishness, from what Griff could figure. After all, it took two to fight.

And it took someone who was willing to give up their "rights" in order to get along.

It wasn't something that most people had any experience in doing.

Chapter 4

"It's pretty hard to do the right thing all the time. Maybe you don't see the struggle that your parents have, or maybe their hearts desire to do right, and they just don't have the character to follow through." Griff stared out at the water.

"A lack of character, that's for sure." Rodney stood beside him.

"Don't you want to be different?" Griff asked. He didn't want to push the kid into doing what he thought he should do. It had to be a choice Rodney made.

"I don't think that's possible. Plus, that's pretty boring. People who live by character don't have any fun."

"Maybe that depends on what your definition of fun is." Griff used to think the exact same thing. That he had to be rebellious, break the rules, do all the bad things in order to have fun. He used to make fun of people who walked the line, did the right thing, were goody-goody people.

And then he figured out that he had everything backward. The only problem was, he wasn't sure that anyone could have told him any different when he was Rodney's age. He had to learn all those things for himself. Thankfully, God had protected him from a lot of bad things. Not everything, but a lot.

"My definition of fun is anything that doesn't have to do with my parents." Rodney sounded even more bitter.

Griff couldn't blame him. If he knew his dad was cheating, he would be upset as well. Of course, Rodney might not know as much as what he thought he did.

"Maybe your parents aren't as bad as what you think."

"Maybe they're worse." Every time Rodney mentioned his dad or his parents, the bitterness crept back into his voice, deep and thick and nasty.

"What makes you think there's an issue?"

"I saw him. Right under your nose too. You've probably seen him too." Rodney gave Griff a nasty glance that almost made him take a step back. And he was just a kid.

"I'm not even sure who your dad is, and I'm in the kitchen most of the time. You mean he's...brought a girlfriend into the diner?"

Honestly, he wouldn't even recognize Rodney's dad. There were a lot of people who came into the diner, and Rodney's dad had never been introduced to Griff. What he said to Rodney was true. He spent a lot of time in the kitchen.

"Just talk to the lady." Rodney said that like he knew Griff would know who he was talking about.

"What lady?" For the first time, a slide of unease went through Griff. He was starting to get an inkling of what Rodney might be talking about.

"You know. The lady. The one you work with. You and she run the diner. She's sleeping with my dad. And he's a married man. It's disgusting."

Chi and the lawyer went through his head. Surely that's not what Rodney was talking about.

He knew she didn't want to be with a married man. Knew she wanted more, but she didn't think she was good enough to deserve anything better than someone who treated her like the lawyer. That was her problem. It wasn't that she didn't have values or morals, she just didn't have a sense of her worth. She didn't understand that it was because God loved her, because God saved her, because God died for her, that gave her worth. Worth that was so far beyond the way that man was treating her.

Could that lawyer, Chi's lawyer, be Rodney's dad?

"Your dad's a lawyer." He said that like a statement, although he was really asking. Because he wasn't sure.

"Yeah. Says he is anyway. I guess I've never really read his degrees. I've been in his office in Chicago a few times, but I never read the stuff on the walls."

"He has an office in Chicago?"

"That's where he works. Sometimes he doesn't come home at night. He's got a penthouse there. Mom never stays there. She works from home all the time. Except when she's taking business trips."

His mom was away, never stayed at the penthouse, worked on her own business.

"Your parents come into Strawberry Sands and eat at the diner?"

"Mom never does. They say Strawberry Sands is too dinky for them. They always go to Blueberry Beach or some swanky suburb of Chicago. But Dad lied about that too. Because I saw him at the diner. I saw him groping that woman." Rodney sneered. "She wasn't telling him no."

Griff grit his teeth. This wasn't supposed to be any of his business. Chi could do whatever she wanted to. Including mess around with a married man. Except... He knew she didn't know the man was married. She thought she was moving in as a precursor to getting a ring. He knew she did.

His heart was heavy. It felt like a dead weight in his chest as his mind whirled, trying to figure out what he could do.

It wasn't just for Chi; he would be able to help Rodney too. Actually, he still really couldn't help Rodney. If the man was going to cheat, he was going to cheat. And he'd find a woman who would cheat with him. Even if he had to lie to her. Which was what Griff was fairly certain Rodney's dad had done to Chi.

He remembered seeing the faint white line on the man's finger that clearly was where a ring usually sat.

Maybe he told Chi he was recently divorced. Maybe that explained the ring. In Chi's mind anyway.

Could he tell Chi that the man she thought she was seeing was married?

What was he going to do if she didn't care?

Did it matter? If he warned her, and she didn't care, then it wasn't on him anymore. But if he knew the information, and he didn't share it, that was on him.

"Just because your dad does something doesn't mean you have to be that way too," he said as he pulled his phone out of his pocket.

"What do you know about that?"

"My dad died in prison." His words were a little absent-minded, because he was texting.

> Where are you?

"No way."

"Yeah. I've worn the black. The skulls and the crossbones. I've done the whole devil thing. And I think it's a lot more powerful and a lot more dangerous than what we realize. You don't have to open your mind to the devil for very long before he eagerly accepts the invitation and jumps in. It's dangerous, far more dangerous than we realize."

"Oh. Scary," Rodney said, and while there was a lot of mocking in his tone, Griff could hear a small note of fear.

"In the Bible, when the Archangel Michael contested with the devil about the body of Moses, he didn't bring an accusation against the devil himself, but he said 'the Lord rebuke you, Satan.' That lets us in on a big secret. That the devil is a lot stronger than what we think he is. Even the Archangel Michael won't mess with him; we definitely shouldn't either."

"I'm not messing with the devil. Not really. But at least he'll take me. No one else seems to want me. I might as well embrace the whole death thing and everything that goes with it."

"I think we don't have an accurate view of hell. It's an eternity of torture and misery. We think we're going to go down to hell to play poker with our buddies, but that's not the way it's going to be." Griff sighed, impatiently tapping his phone. No text had come back.

"Sure it is. You don't know. You've never been there."

"The Bible says it's not. The Bible tells us about a man who was in torment. He was so thirsty he was dying for someone to dip the tip of their finger into some water to cool his tongue. He was begging for that. It's pain and misery, and you're not there with your friends. You're alone. You don't even know that there are other people there unless you hear them screaming in agony. It's not a place you want to go. It's not a place you want to mess with. Satan is the great deceiver. He's going to convince you that he loves you, but he doesn't."

"Nobody does."

"God does. And that's one of Satan's lies to tell you that He doesn't. That He couldn't. That something that you've done is too bad, or that if your parents don't love you, God can't love you either. I'm telling you, Satan lies."

"How do you know?" Rodney seemed like he was listening, even though he stared belligerently at the lake, his arms crossed over his chest.

"Because the Bible tells us he's a liar and the father of it. That's why it's so terrible when people lie. Instead of being like God, they're being like Satan. And that helps Satan win."

"If God is so strong, He could beat Satan Himself."

"He can. But don't you like to watch your team win? Does it make you feel good when your team has a victory? If you can do something for God to have a victory, wouldn't you want to do that? Wouldn't you want to make Him feel good? But when you do sinful things, you're giving Satan the victory. You're making him feel good. You're letting him have the power to gloat and say something along the lines of, 'How about that, God? There's your boy. Look at him, he's fighting for my team.' Do you want to allow Satan to do that with you? That he uses your actions to gloat in God's face about how one of God's children is playing for the wrong team?"

Griff took a steadying breath. He didn't typically talk that much, but Rodney was definitely playing fast and loose. He didn't understand how powerful the spirit world was. Didn't understand that when a person opened their mind to anything that had to do with that, even if it was music that was played by people who were Satan worshipers, they were opening their mind to things they didn't understand. It seemed simple and innocent, but that was only because of humans' limited ability to see. God wouldn't have warned them so strongly away from witches and necromancers and anything that had to do with people who dealt with the dead, if He hadn't known for a fact that those things were bad for humans.

He didn't want to see Rodney go down that path. Griff still had scars from when he had been caught in that world.

"It's boring to play for the good guys."

"Don't you want to play for the winning team?" He didn't know how else to try to convince Rodney.

"Not really. God allowed my dad to cheat on my mom, to blow up my family."

"God allowed that? Why aren't you going to put the blame where it belongs? Satan allowed that. Satan tempted your dad away. Satan lied to your dad and told him that he'd be happier if he were screwing around with some other woman. Satan's lies are what have blown up your family. God is waiting for you to turn back to Him so He can try to put things back together. He's waiting for your dad to do the same."

Lord, help him understand. Help him to see You love him.

Griff prayed, even as he twisted his phone in his hand, flipping it over and over, praying for Chi, asking God to save her from wherever she was and help her to see that she was doing the wrong thing too.

Griff couldn't do it on his own. He couldn't fix her, couldn't save her, couldn't even get to her because he didn't know where she was. But God knew.

"Why can't God just fix everything if He's so powerful?"

That was a good question. Sometimes Griff wished God would reach down and force people to do what they should do, instead of what they wanted.

"I wish," he said honestly and maybe more fervently than he should have. After all, he was thinking about Chi. He wished God would make her do right. Make her fall in love with Griff instead of chasing after some lawyer who was hiding the fact that he was already married with a kid.

"That's not the way God set the world up to work. And it's not the way you would want it either, if you think about it. You don't want people to like you because they're forced to. You don't want people to do things for you because they have to.

"You want people to choose to be kind to you. You want people to choose to be with you. You want people to choose to love you. God's the same way. What fun is it if He forces everyone to love Him? He wants them to come to Him of their own free will."

He sighed. "Eventually, the Bible says every knee will bow and every tongue will confess that Jesus Christ is Lord. That means eventually God will stop giving us free choice, and He will force us to worship Him. We won't have a choice at that point. But He wants us to come to Him while we're still able to do it ourselves. He wants us to make that choice, to choose to love and serve Him on our own. It means so much more."

"I guess I don't care if my dad chooses to love me or not. I just want him to. I'm perfectly fine if God has to force him to."

Those were honest words, and Griff figured Rodney probably didn't mean to say them. That was his heart. He just wanted his dad to love him. And it was sad.

Griff couldn't take the place of his dad, no one could. But he could try to help him. Had been.

Before he got a chance to say anything more, his phone buzzed. He flipped it over, looking at the text immediately.

> I'm driving to Chicago, why?

> I need to talk to you.

He wanted to say *don't text while you're driving*, but he needed to know where she was going. What she was doing.

> Tomorrow. Tonight I'm checking out the Chicago Museum of Fine Arts.

Had he heard that there was some kind of gala there? It seemed like maybe Chi had mentioned it a time or two, and she probably heard it from her lawyer friend, which was why Griff had tuned her out. In fact, he remembered her complaining that her lawyer friend was going without her and wondering if she wasn't good enough to go to something fancy like that.

He blew out a breath. If tomorrow was the earliest he could see Chi, he'd take her up on it. But there was no point in texting her again.

He didn't like to admit defeat, and there was a nagging thought in his brain.

Go to her tonight.

He didn't have anything that was suitable to wear to a gala at the Chicago Museum of Fine Arts. He couldn't go to that.

Go tonight.

Was that the Lord? Or was that just him wanting to go, to try to save Chi before it was too late? Although, he supposed there was no such thing as too late. Unless she died. And he didn't think the lawyer wanted to kill her. He just wanted to use her, use her innocence or her lack of knowledge against her. String her along, letting her think that she was going to be getting a ring, putting her up in some penthouse as his mistress, without her really even realizing it. Thinking she was the only woman in his life and the woman he would eventually be marrying.

"Will you do me a favor and think about what I said?"

"You said a lot today. Normally you don't talk that much. I should have been taking notes." Rodney's voice was back to being sarcastic and bitter.

"I guess I could tell you from personal experience."

He really didn't want to talk about that part of his past. He worked hard to let it go. He stepped away from everything. After he'd worked his way to the very top, thinking that would fill his soul. But there was nothing that would satisfy a soul outside Jesus. And he was a lot happier out of the rat race.

Except, Chi seemed to want someone who was winning the rat race.

The thought made him sad, because she was deceived as well.

He couldn't fix anyone. Couldn't convince Rodney that he was thinking the wrong thing. Couldn't save Chi from making the worst decision of her life. It made him wonder if he could even save himself.

He couldn't. Only God could.

I need faith, Lord. I'm feeling the need to do this myself. I don't want to just let things go. Help me.

Go to Chicago. Tonight.

He almost looked around, the words felt so real.

"I need to go. I want to talk to you some more though." He put a hand on Rodney's shoulder, and to his surprise, Rodney allowed it. Maybe Rodney had a little bit more respect for him than what he let on. Or maybe he just was so desperate for an adult to take interest in and care about him that anyone would do.

Whichever it was, Griff would take it.

"Where are you going?" Rodney asked, and Griff almost thought that there was a little bit of fear in his eyes, like he didn't want to be alone.

"I think I need to take a ride to Chicago."

"I see." Although it was clear that Rodney didn't see.

"I know it's warmer than it usually is," he said, thinking it was kind of unbelievable that it was the first week in December. But they had those types of days, few and far between in the winter, where the temperatures were unseasonably warm. "But the temps are supposed to drop, and there's a storm moving in. Make sure you're home, okay? It's supposed to be a bad one."

He heard they were going to get more snow than they usually got this early in the season, if the winds blew just right, with the cold front that was coming out of Canada.

Still, it would be warm enough for him to ride his bike to Chicago, and he shouldn't have too much trouble getting back, although by nine or so, the temps would be dropping. They were supposed to drop fast. So he couldn't spend a whole lot of time there, but he'd have enough time to at least get a few sentences out to Chi. Whether she believed him, whether she didn't, that was going to be up to the Lord.

Chapter 5

Chi looked around the room, crowded with people laughing and mingling. The laughter sounded fake, the mingling forced. There was lots of makeup, lots of updos that probably took hours to create, dresses that cost more money than she'd seen in her entire life, men with suave smiles and calculating eyes.

She didn't belong here.

It was unseasonably warm outside, and the maintenance people at the big, swanky building must have had trouble keeping up, because sweat dripped down the small of her back and down her temple as well. She tried to unobtrusively brush it away, praying she wasn't messing up her makeup.

This was the world she wanted to belong to. These were the people she wanted to have accept her. They all seemed so confident and put together. Fake, yes, but obviously they had money and prestige, and that gave them a leg up in the world.

She wanted that for herself. For her children. For the rest of her life, she wanted to be able to give the people she loved what they wanted, because of her position and power.

Where was James?

Her pink dress felt out of place amidst all the darker colors. Blacks and navy blues and reds. There were some whites and creams, but nothing pink and frilly like what she had on.

It was a dress she'd bought to go to the last wedding she attended, several years ago. Thankfully it still fit. And even more thankfully, it was warm outside, so she didn't freeze in it. It looked like spring and said high school prom.

But hopefully no one noticed. Surely they weren't surveying the room, looking for a dress that was completely out of place.

There had to be people who were doing that. There always were. But hopefully she'd find James, and once she was on his arm, people wouldn't dare say anything unkind about her or her dress.

He'd mentioned how respected he was as a Chicago lawyer, and people wouldn't dare talk bad about whatever woman was on his arm. And she intended for that to be her.

A waiter walked by, and she took a piece of whatever it was that was on his tray, picking it up by the toothpick that was stuck in it. Rice wrapped in some green stuff with... It looked like raw chicken, but she knew a person couldn't eat raw chicken, so it couldn't be that. She stuck it in her mouth.

She only chewed once before she frantically looked for a garbage can, making a mental note to not take anything off any tray again. Not until James was by her side to tell her what it was.

She was pretty sure that it looked like raw chicken because it was raw chicken.

Or maybe raw fish. Wasn't sushi supposed to be raw fish?

She owned a diner, but they didn't sell anything that fancy. Hamburgers and French fries were simple and hardy and kept the people in Strawberry Sands content.

These people were in a totally different class. She found a trash can and spit the offending bite of raw meat out of her mouth.

"Excuse me?" She spoke to another woman, who somehow managed to turn around and look down her nose at her and let her know how annoyed she was to be bothered, without saying a word.

"Never mind. Sorry," Chi said, looking for someone who seemed friendly and nice.

Maybe it was where she was standing, but she couldn't see a single person who fit that description.

Her dress felt too tight, too low, too exposing.

She glanced around, saw that there was no one looking at her, and then took both hands, holding the toothpick between her first two fingers like a cigarette, and pulled her dress up as hard as she could.

It felt like her boobs were about ready to fall out of it. She hated that feeling. She was already nervous enough, because she wasn't supposed to be here.

James had specifically said that he wasn't taking her.

But it was because he had business in the morning and he wouldn't be able to bring her home.

She felt like he was trying to push her into moving in with him. After all, if they lived together, he wouldn't have to worry about taking her home.

If that had been his end goal, it had been successful.

Her heart shriveled a little, the way it did every time she thought about moving in with James. No matter how much time she spent trying to convince herself that she wanted to, that it didn't matter, that everyone did it, that she would be fine, she hadn't been able to get rid of that feeling. The feeling that it was wrong. Some people might call it her conscience, maybe it was, but it felt more like the Holy Spirit whispering to her that she didn't want to sin like that.

If a person truly had the Lord in their life, they couldn't just wink at sin. They couldn't accept it, they couldn't continue to live it or walk into it with their eyes wide open. The Holy Spirit would let them know that it was wrong.

The feeling had gone from a little bit of unease to whispered words to what felt like God shouting in her head that she couldn't go through with it.

Maybe she should go outside, get back in her car, and drive back to Strawberry Sands before the storm hit.

Chicagoans were quite savvy about the weather. They were used to big snows, lots of wind, and winter temps.

They just adjusted their plans and went on living.

Chi had moved through the entire building and found herself back at the door when a gust of cold air blew in.

Several ladies around her gasped, and it made Chi turn toward the dark night that the open door exposed.

She thought she caught a glimpse of James.

But it couldn't have been James, because that man had a woman in a red dress beside him.

Still, her feet took her in that direction, waiting for the door to open again. They had been walking her way, the woman's gloved hand on his arm, her sparkling eyes looking up at him and laughing at something he'd said.

Somehow that image became burned into her brain.

But the man's face was blurring in her head. It looked a little bit like James, but it wasn't him. It couldn't be. Surely not.

But the unease that had been plaguing her, that had made her take off and come without being invited, shot to life.

Her brain said that she had been a fool, and she needed to keep her eyes on the door.

Her heart told her to trust everything that James had said, because he was a good man. Sometimes she thought her heart was the stupidest organ in her body.

She was just a few feet from the door when it opened again.

She froze.

It was James. It was definitely James. And yes, he had a woman in red beside him. He looked down on her with affection, with the same look that he looked at Chi with. He looked at her like that in the diner when she sat down beside him, tired and aching, her feet hurting, her ankles swollen.

He said to her that she shouldn't work so hard, that she should come away with him.

She'd always resisted. She didn't want to live with someone, she wanted to be married to him. She wanted to mean enough that he made a commitment, a lifetime commitment, to her.

She wasn't just a trial or someone to keep his bed warm until he found someone he liked better.

The woman stood at the door, taking off her wrap, as a man in a smart black suit waited for her to hand it to him. He stood back and to the side, not stealing any of the spotlight from the beautiful lady.

Was that a Hollywood actress?

She looked a little different in person than on screen. Her hair was a slightly different color, but Chi was pretty sure that woman was a movie star. Maybe not the highest-paid, most popular one, but one she'd seen on TV. She was almost certain she was.

What was James doing at a diner in a tiny town paying attention to the waitress in the diner, when he had a movie star on his arm?

But she knew. She knew exactly what James had wanted with her. And she knew now that there had been no marriage in her future.

At least he wasn't married himself. That would've been far, far worse.

Except... Maybe he was.

He had told her he was divorced, but everything else he had said was a lie. Maybe that was a lie too. Maybe she wasn't the only one that had been deceived, since the movie star on his arm laughed up into his face like she actually liked him.

Chi glanced down, down where his hand lay wrapped around the woman's waist. No ring. Just that faint white band, like sometimes there was a ring.

Somehow, as she stood there, whether or not he was married was the question that burned in her mind. She was jealous of that woman he had on his arm, upset with herself for even being there, and part of her wanted to duck away without him seeing her at all. Knowing how pathetic she was. Knowing that she had followed him the whole way to Chicago. Suspecting that she was there to move in. She was going to debase herself like that. But a big part of her wanted to know, needed to know, had to know, whether or not James was married.

Had she been messing around with another woman's husband?

Taking a breath, trying to push back the shades of red that were shrouding her vision, she walked, no, she stomped, over to the man who had been whispering sweet nothings in her ear just yesterday at the diner.

"James. Imagine meeting you here."

She could tell immediately he recognized her voice. Because he froze. He had been in the middle of saying something to the woman in red, but his voice trailed off as her words penetrated in his head.

She could wait. Let them penetrate.

Slowly he turned his head, and his eyes focused on hers.

She thought he was going to deny even knowing her. She wasn't going to let that happen. Putting her hands on her hips, she lifted her eyes, gave him her most haughty look, and said in her most cultured voice, "James Connolly, are you married?"

He laughed, derisively, insultingly, like she was a child who had asked if Santa Claus was real, demanded that her parents tell her.

But the woman beside him stopped. Her eyes went to Chi, and her brows furrowed.

"Connolly?" And she tilted her head, as though there was something wrong.

"James Connolly. That's who you're with." Chi smiled smugly. "Why? Did he give you a different name?"

"Flanagan. He said his name was James Flanagan. I looked him up. He practices law in Chicago just like he said."

"I looked him up too, and James Connolly practices law in Chicago. So, I guess he lied to you."

"Or to you," the woman said, regaining her equilibrium, as she lifted an elegantly arched brow. The look she gave Chi was designed to put her back in her place.

Part of Chi wanted to go back and crawl under the rock she should never have come out of. He hadn't even given her his real name.

Or he'd lied to the woman in red. One of the two.

Anger, fierce and sharp, swept through her, lighting her on fire, causing the red haze that had obscured her vision to darken and shimmer.

She'd never wanted to claw someone's eyes out so bad in her life before. This man had been lying to her for months. He led her along, invited her to live with him, and everything he said had been a lie.

"I trusted you!"

She wanted to call him names, tell him what a low-down dirty rotten sneak he was, wanted to slap him, wanted to hurt the woman beside him, even though logically she knew it wasn't her fault. But the desire to hurt someone else the way she had been hurt was strong.

Mostly she felt stupid.

And worthless. Used. And totally and completely unloved and unlovely.

She barely noticed the blast of air that shot over her as the door opened again. Her eyes were focused solely on James, whatever his name was. He didn't even look contrite. He only looked concerned that the woman in red beside him believed him.

She wanted his attention back on her.

"Are you married?" she asked, not shouting, but her words were loud enough to cause several conversations that were nearby to stop as people craned their heads to look.

"You're going to make a scene," James said, talking to her like she was a child. It made her mad. Even more angry than what she already was, but logically, she knew there was no point. She would only make herself look bad, while James would walk away, spinning everything so that he looked like the victim, instead of the lying jerk he was.

Her heart beat wildly, and her breath came in gasps as she tried to figure out what she could say that would wound him, put him in his place where he belonged, show him how little he meant to her.

But there was nothing. Because she was the fool who had fallen for his lies. She was the one who had believed him. And the reason she had was because she wanted to move up in the world. She wanted more than what she had. She wasn't content with what God had given her, she wanted more. Wanted power and prestige and money and all the things that came with being on the arm of a handsome, wealthy, successful man.

She was here, because of her greed and sin and stupidity.

She saw that just as clearly as she saw that nothing she said would make any difference at all.

"He's very convincing. I guess I'd be careful if I were you," she said, looking at the woman in red, pity swirling through her, replacing the anger. Pity for that woman, pity for James who obviously wasn't content with what he had either but wanted multiple women on his arms, on his string, in his house or bed or whatever.

The idea sickened her. That she had almost fallen for that. If she had decided to come stay, she would have. Now, she just needed to turn and walk away, and try not to show how embarrassed and ashamed and stupid she felt.

"Chi?" The deep voice touched every nerve ending she had in her body and somehow made her heart feel like it was lifted up off the floor and set back in her chest properly.

"Griff?" she said, looking around, sure she recognized that voice.

Sure enough, there he stood. Leather jacket over top of a white T-shirt. Worn blue jeans, and those boots he'd worn every day she'd seen him since she'd known him.

His bald head glistened under the gala lights, and he set his shades on top of his head, so his ice-blue eyes drilled into hers.

The way he looked at her made her feel like she was the only woman in the room. Like she wasn't wearing a frilly high school-like dress, didn't feel out of place, but that she totally belonged and he admired and respected her.

He always made her feel like that. Like she could do more than what she thought she could, just because he thought she could do it.

Funny how Griff had the ability to make her feel that way. No one else ever did.

Not even James.

"You coming with me?" he asked, as she tried to remember when she felt the blast of air. How much of this had he seen?

She supposed he didn't need to have seen any of it. All he needed to do was look over and recognize James as the liar who had been at the diner multiple times, giving her attention, and she had been lapping it up.

Was she going with Griff?

Unlike James, Griff had never lied to her. In fact, as she stood there, the seconds slowly ticking by, she realized that since the day Griff had walked into her diner, he had never stopped trying to do what was best for her. He had worked alongside of her, put in just as many hours as she had, worked to make the diner profitable, figured out recipes that the town would love, and he had done it all while being kind and respectful to her and helping her any way he could.

Maybe she'd taken him for granted. More than a little.

And now, somehow he'd asked where she was and had shown up just when she needed him. She allowed a little smile to curve up her lips, even though the inside of her chest still hadn't eased. Pain, disgust, disappointment, all mixed with something that felt a lot like...trust. Griff was someone she could trust. Especially at a time like this, when the rest of her world seemed to be turning upside down.

"Yes."

Her word made him smile just a little, although his taciturn nature did not allow his lips to turn up more than a fraction of an inch.

His hand stretched out, and she looked down.

Without thinking about it, she reached out and put her hand into his.

"Let's go home," he said, his eyes meeting hers. To her surprise, there seemed to be a question in them. Home? Was he talking about the diner?

It seemed like an odd thing to say, but she nodded, squeezed his hand, and followed him as he walked out the door.

Chapter 6

She had come.

Griff couldn't believe it. He felt like he had risked everything by walking in and asking Chi to go with him.

He'd seen there was a big scene, that Chi had to have seen that the lawyer was at least with someone else, even if she didn't realize he was married. He doubted the woman that man was with was his wife. But Griff really didn't know.

Regardless, Chi had chosen him and had taken his hand.

He led her out of the door and down the stairs.

He'd parked his bike right at the edge of the sidewalk, and the valet had immediately pulled out his phone and called a tow.

Thankfully, he hadn't spent much time inside, and the tow truck hadn't gotten there.

"I wasn't sure whether we'd still have a ride or not," he murmured as he led her to his bike.

"I have my car, but I'm not sure I can drive right now. I feel like I need time to think." Her words were soft and a little sad, and they made his heart squeeze.

"We'll come back for it," he said, wanting to say so much more than that but not knowing how to say the other things he wanted to.

"Thanks for coming. You've been a good friend. I didn't realize just how good, until we were standing in there. I haven't appreciated you the way I should."

No. No. He was not her friend. Well, he was, but he didn't want her to friend-zone him. He wanted more. He wanted her to see that he was there, yes because he liked her as a friend, but because he liked her for so much more, and he wanted her to realize she liked him the same way.

Was he going to come all this way, take her home, and have nothing change?

He knew it didn't matter. He would do it anyway. He loved her.

"Wear my helmet," he said, handing it to her.

She looked at it like she'd never put a motorcycle helmet on before.

"Here," he said, grinning a little.

"So now he smiles?" she asked, looking at his lips.

Not with any kind of passion, just with surprise, like she'd never seen him smile before. Maybe she hadn't. He did have a tendency to be serious, especially since he pulled himself out of so much garbage.

So all he had to do to get her to look at his lips was smile? He'd do it more often, then.

"It's just a helmet; it's not a space suit."

"I've got a feeling I'm going to wish it was. It's hot out now, but it's supposed to get cold shortly."

"And snow. We're supposed to get a lot of snow."

She sighed. "That's winter."

She'd never complained about the snow before. Maybe it was just the idea that her life was changing, and she didn't have much of anything to look forward to. Or she felt she didn't anyway.

He pulled the helmet from her hand, flipped it over, and set it down on top of her head. She lifted her chin for him, and he buckled it, careful not to pinch the delicate skin of her neck. He pulled the strap until it was snug but not tight.

"How does that feel?"

"Like I'm ready to jump into a foxhole in France."

He snorted. "No foxholes. Hopefully this is just for show, but it will make me feel better if you have it on."

"Where's yours?"

He nodded to the one she wore. "Never needed a second one." That was the truth.

For some reason, that made her smile. Then he understood when she spoke.

"That's nice to know. Apparently James had at least one other woman, and I suspect he is married."

"He is."

Her brows went way up, then they pulled down and her eyes narrowed.

"You knew, and you didn't tell me?" Her words were spit out, like she'd gone from zero to massively angry in just one second.

"I just found out. That's the reason I'm here. I was going to tell you. I texted you while I was talking to his son."

"He has a son?"

Out of the corner of his eye, Griff could see the valet walking toward them.

"We need to scoot. I... I was going to take you to my cabin in Raspberry Ridge. It's rather primitive, but it will be a place to lie low for a day or two until you get yourself pulled together."

She nodded, her brow still not straightening out, like she still hadn't quite gotten over the idea that James was married and Griff had known about it.

He was sure she believed him when he said he just found out. She just needed a little bit of time to process. That was most likely a pretty big surprise for her.

"I'm fine with whatever."

"All right. Let me get on first." He threw his leg over, after pulling the key out of his pocket.

"Want help?" He looked at her as she stood on the sidewalk, biting her lip.

"I'm gonna put a hand on your shoulder."

"Okay."

She did, using him to steady herself, and he liked that. Liked that she trusted him to be solid under her and give her the balance she needed. He wanted to be there for her every day. In every way.

One thing at a time. He just had to take it one thing at a time.

Chapter 7

Chi shivered on the back of Griff's bike.

He'd stopped about an hour out of Chicago, when the wind had started gusting and the temperature had started dropping, and given her his leather jacket.

He just wore a thin T-shirt now as she pressed against him, loving how he felt warm and substantial under her hands. He was not a thin man. She wouldn't call him fat, but his chest was thick, his stomach maybe a little pouchy, but in a very good way. At least, she appreciated the fact that he blocked most of the wind, and she could hide behind him, holding on tight, taking his warmth and protection.

She didn't know how cold it was, but she assumed that it was freezing or below as the first flurries had started to fall.

They'd passed the sign for Strawberry Sands just a few miles ago, and then Griff had turned his bike off the interstate at a little-used exit that declared the town of Raspberry Ridge was just ahead.

Even though she'd lived in Strawberry Sands for years, she hadn't ever been to Raspberry Ridge.

They were far enough north that there were trees, even though the ground was still flat. Several cabins dotted the area, and as they motored closer, she could see a glimpse of the lake and realized they were riding alongside of it.

It felt secluded and safe.

Interestingly, when she was thinking about going to James's penthouse, living with him, she hadn't felt safe. And it definitely hadn't felt right.

Of course, she wasn't moving in with Griff, just going to his house, but it didn't put off alarm bells in her head the way being alone with James had. Even though she had been attracted to James.

Griff was just her friend.

He had been a good friend to her. On the ride to his cabin, she determined that she was going to be just as good a friend to him as he had been to her. Starting today.

"Just a bit further." The wind blew Griff's words past her ears as he turned his head just a bit and spoke.

She nodded her head and then realized he couldn't see her. "Okay."

He slowed down even more, glancing behind him before he turned left onto a gravel road, carefully maneuvering the bike over the stones.

The trees opened up, and a majestic view of the lake stretched out before them. A small cabin, one that looked barely bigger than a one room, maybe two, sat at the back of the clearing.

The opening stretched right to a cliff, where the ground dropped out of sight.

She knew Lake Michigan had cliffs as well as sandy beaches, but she hadn't seen anything like this before.

"This is amazing," she breathed, meaning it. It was all the more amazing as the large snowflakes that had been falling drifted past the cliff's edge. It hindered her view, which she supposed was even more spectacular when the clouds weren't lowered and the snow wasn't falling.

Still, it gave a cozy glow to everything, even if the cabin was dark.

Night had long since fallen, along with the temperatures, and she realized that she really hadn't been a very good friend after all. If she had, she would have insisted that Griff take his jacket back. After all, he was the one who was blocking the wind.

"You have to be cold."

"I've felt worse. But I'll be warm soon enough. I know I need to split some wood before I can build a fire, and that will be job number one."

"Split wood?"

He shut the bike off and kicked the stand down, allowing it to slowly tilt until it rested on the kickstand. "Yeah. There's no electricity or heat other than a woodstove. It's too remote."

"Oh my goodness. No electricity?"

"There is a pump, it's in the cabin, and it's working. I was there last week. To check it."

"All right. So we have water?"

"Yeah. We'll have heat here in a little bit. And there is a cellular signal, although there is no internet, of course."

"Of course. And I can't charge my phone."

"Not right now."

Just then, a gust of wind blew, swirling flakes, reminding Chi that she was cold and Griff had to be colder. There was a bit of moonlight seeping through the storm clouds, just enough to see by, but it was as chilly as the sunlight had been warm earlier that day.

"You can have your jacket back."

"No. You keep it. I... I guess I should have thought to stop and get some clothes for us."

She hadn't thought of that either. "Yeah. I hate this dress."

"I think it's cute," he said, swinging a leg up and over the bike and twisting so she saw the little smile on his face.

If it was anyone else, she would have thought he was making fun of her.

"I'll tell you what, I'll trade you. You give me your jeans and T-shirt, and you can have the dress if you like it so much."

"It's cute on you," he corrected himself. "On me, it would look hideous."

"You're not going to get me to argue with that."

"I think I have a few extra flannels and some sweatpants inside. We'll see what's there. It's not going to be the Hilton, but it'll be better than a tepee."

"All right. Better than a tepee. I don't think that's going to sell anything, but it's nice to know."

He held out a hand, and she put her hand in his, allowing him to help her off the bike and finding that her legs felt like they could barely support her.

Thankfully, he didn't let go of her hand as they started walking toward the cabin.

"There's no lock on the door, and the outhouse is out back."

"Outhouse?"

"Maybe I shouldn't have brought you here."

"No. This is exactly the right place for me to…lick my wounds, I guess." She didn't want to get into it right now. And while she would prefer to have electricity and hot water, and internet, she supposed a day or two at this cabin would be just what she needed.

He didn't look like he was convinced, and his lips flattened. Then, he looked out over the cliff, at the sky and the lake and the snow flurries that fell softly to the ground.

"I'm afraid we don't have much choice. It is uncomfortable to drive the bike when it's cold out, but it's impossible to drive it when it's snowing. We'd never make it back to Strawberry Sands."

"We're stuck here?" she asked, suddenly feeling far less comfortable than she had just seconds ago.

He smiled. "My phone still works, and yours does too. As long as we don't run out of battery, we can call anyone we want to. I know we both have friends in Strawberry Sands who would come get us in a heartbeat. And," he jerked his head toward the cliff, "I built the cabin here because of the view, but there's a trail that takes you down to the beach. It would be about a ten-mile walk, but we can get to Strawberry Sands."

"Oh. Just ten miles?"

"That's it."

They grinned at each other, both of them knowing that ten miles was more than just a little walk. But it would be doable in an emergency. It made her feel less isolated.

"I do have a generator, and we can run it if we need to charge our phones. I do have a hot water heater as well, and it will run that, although if we can wait and heat the water on the woodstove, that would be best."

"All right. I… I can go in and…" She took a breath. "Do you have food?"

"Well, as much as I think that you're probably right, coming up here and fasting is a good idea… Yes, I have food."

"All right then. I'll go in and make us something to eat."

"Sounds good. I have a list of recipes on the table that I was going to try the next time I came up. I have all the ingredients for them stocked in the pantry and in the ice chest out back."

So he'd been planning on spending some time here. That was interesting. He worked just as hard as she did, and they both put in twice the hours that a normal person put in every week for the last several years.

She hadn't even realized he had a cabin. She thought he spent all of his spare time in the apartment above the diner.

Shows what she knew.

She had to admit, she was more wrapped up in herself than she should have been. Again she thought about what a terrible friend she had been.

The wind gusted once more, and she pulled his leather jacket tighter around herself before she peeled it off.

"It's too cold for you to be out here without this."

"I told you, I'll be chopping wood soon, and it'll just end up sitting on the stump beside me."

"Well, wear it until then," she said, knowing that she should have given it to him a long time ago.

"Go ahead and take it in with you. I don't really want it to get wet anyway." He looked up at the sky. "From what I understand, it's just going to get worse. I'll probably be a little bit, I want to make sure I have enough to keep us warm all night."

"That sounds good to me. I like the idea of being warm all night."

He grinned. "Go on in and make yourself at home."

She nodded, somehow almost feeling happy. Maybe it was his small grin, the one she hadn't seen much at all in the time that they'd worked together, the one she'd seen more today than in all that time.

Or maybe it was because she knew she dodged a bullet. She could have been with James Connolly, or whatever his name was, right now. And that would be terrible. There definitely was a part of her that was sad, a little heartbroken. But it was more because of the fact that her dreams had been lost. Not because she was so madly in love with James.

She realized that now. She hadn't really even liked him. What she had liked was the idea of him. The idea of having someone to give her respectability.

She almost laughed as she turned away, walking toward the cabin.

As he said, the door was unlocked. She glanced both ways at the front porch, noting the rocking chairs and the railing. It looked like Griff might have made it all himself. She'd have to ask.

He didn't look like the kind of person who would know how to cook, but obviously it was something he either enjoyed or spent time doing, even in his spare time, since he'd said that he had the ingredients to try out some new recipes.

So, maybe building cabins was something else he had in his repertoire that no one who looked at him would ever guess.

She almost laughed. Griff was a study in contradictions. Or surprises. She certainly hadn't expected him to come the whole way to Chicago...for her.

That did something to her woman's heart. She just realized he had driven two hours knowing there was a snowstorm on the way, just so he could...warn her?

Why didn't he text her the information?

But she knew why. She probably wouldn't have listened. She needed to see what she had seen, needed to have Griff standing in front of her. Maybe he knew what was going down and arrived to pick up the pieces.

Maybe Griff cared about her more than what she realized.

The thought made her pause, and she closed the door and stood in front of it. At first, she didn't see the interior of the cabin, because she was so focused on wondering whether she could be right about that. Did Griff truly care about her more than what she realized?

She tucked that idea away to think about later. There was something...exciting in that thought.

It was too dark to see anything; the moonlight wasn't strong enough to penetrate the deeper darkness of the cabin. She pulled up the flashlight app on her phone, worried a bit about its battery life but not wanting to bump into anything until she got a feel for the layout.

The interior of the cabin didn't offer too many surprises. There were several sheets of paper on the small table as Griffin had said, a small amount of what looked like butcher block counters. Perhaps they were handmade as well. A sink, but instead of a spigot, a well pump stuck out of it. Interesting. She'd never seen anything quite like that, but she thought she could probably use it. She'd used a well pump before. Back in Ohio. Those days were so long ago she could barely believe she was the same person, but it wouldn't be too hard for her to remember some of the things she knew. Using a well pump being one of them.

There was a refrigerator, which surprised her. There was no electricity in the cabin. Then she realized that maybe it was gas. She hadn't known there was such a thing. As her eyes moved forward, she saw the woodstove. She'd used one of those back in the day.

It wasn't going to be quite as primitive as what she thought.

Well, she probably wouldn't be any good chopping wood, but she could have some food ready for Griff when he came in. He said he was going to be a while, so she didn't feel any need to rush but walked over to the table, looked at the papers, and chose the chicken corn chowder. He'd already made a version of that at the diner, although this one looked a little different. He said he had all the ingredients, so she decided to go ahead and give it a go.

Determined not to fail in at least cooking for the man who had been so good for her, she grabbed the paper and got to work.

Chapter 8

He shouldn't have brought her here. What was he thinking? He should have taken her to the new house that he just closed on. It had every comfort known to man, big windows overlooking the lake, heat, electricity, internet, and several spare bedrooms. A big chef's kitchen, and tons of space. It almost screamed wealth and luxury.

He'd bought it...but maybe he shouldn't have. It was the first thing he'd bought since he came to Strawberry Sands. He'd been allowing his investments to accumulate wealth and putting a little bit of his money aside every month. He didn't make much at the diner, but he didn't really need much. The small apartment over the diner was included with his job. All he had to pay was electricity and the internet and his phone bill.

He lived simply and hadn't touched any of his savings. It felt good to pay for things in cash. No one who knew him when he was a kid would have thought that he would be where he was at this point in his life.

Maybe he liked it that way. Maybe he liked not living the way he could but living the way he wanted to.

Regardless, he had brought Chi here, and he wasn't sure why.

She was going to be roughing it in the worst way. No electricity, uncertain heat, water she had to warm on the stove, and just one bedroom.

Of course she could have it, and he would be sleeping right outside on the rather hard couch.

It wasn't long enough for him, and it wasn't comfortable either, from the little bit of time he'd spent on it.

Typically, he sat on the rocking chairs on the porch.

He didn't spend much time here in the winter.

Regardless, it was what it was.

And he knew, even if he didn't want to admit it, most likely the reason he was here and not at his bigger house was because he wanted Chi to be stuck with him. He didn't want to drop her off at her house and then go home to his.

She hadn't even questioned him. But she probably would, sooner rather than later. After all, why couldn't he have just dropped her off at her house?

He told her he was taking her here, and she hadn't thought to argue. But she'd just been through a very big shock, and her brain probably wasn't working correctly.

As soon as it kicked into gear again, she was going to demand to know what was going on with him. Why had he wanted her here?

And he had no idea what he was going to say. He could hardly tell her that he just wanted to spend time with her. Just wanted to be with her. Just wanted...her to see that he was more than her cook and all-around general helper at the diner.

Of course, he wasn't sure how he thought them being here together would show her any of that. If she hadn't seen it in the last few years they worked together, there was certainly no guarantee that she was going to see it now.

He went to the small shed and grabbed the ax from where he had stored it.

He hadn't cut any firewood since he'd used it all in the spring.

He meant to make it out all summer long, but they'd been busy at the diner, and he hadn't been too inspired to do much of anything, because he'd been moping about the fact that Chi seemed more and more infatuated with that lawyer.

The labor felt good, the rhythm that he fell into as he split the billets he'd cut last winter giving his mind a break from all the things he was thinking about. Just setting up the piece of wood, splitting it neatly in half, picking up the pieces and stacking them. Good, honest labor that, as he had told Chi, warmed him up in no time.

Several hours had gone by, and at least two inches of snow lay on the ground before he grabbed an armful of wood and carried it over to the porch.

He made several trips like that, with armfuls of wood, until he had enough to last the night. Even if it got down below zero, they would be fine.

The cabin was snug and cozy, and once he got a fire going, they would be toasty warm.

She would want to keep her bedroom door open, just so the heat could drift in, but beyond that, it would be just as snug as being in a house with electricity. Even more so probably.

He loved the smell of the woodstove and usually really enjoyed the time he got to spend here.

He hardly thought that Chi would enjoy it. This was the kind of thing, simple and peaceful, that he enjoyed. Chi was always about prestige and whatever security or looks she felt like she got from her lawyer.

Griff supposed not everybody had learned the way he had years ago that that stuff didn't mean anything. It was just as empty as the life he lived before that. Maybe not as dangerous, but empty all the same.

But maybe Chi would have done a lot of good with the money that she would have gotten. Maybe she would still find someone who would give her that life. Maybe she just needed to regroup and refocus her efforts on someone else.

With that thought, he picked up the last armful of wood, carried it onto the back porch, and walked in the door. He'd avoided her long enough; it was time that he faced up to what he had done.

Chapter 9

When Griff dumped the first armload of wood on the back porch, it startled Chi.

She hadn't considered that she wouldn't be able to actually cook anything until he came in and started a fire. Instead, not wanting to waste her phone's battery, she'd turned off the flashlight app and settled down in a chair to wait.

Time passed, with nothing but the muffled thump of axe on wood to mark it, and Chi dozed off until the sudden clatter of wood just outside the door shook her awake. Blinking sleepily, she stretched stiff limbs, then walked out and saw the wood.

She'd already found matches, and she supposed she could try her hand at starting a fire.

The stove had been cleaned out, so she looked around for a little bit of kindling.

Seeing the box off in the corner of the porch, she grabbed a few small pieces, along with a couple hunks of wood, and took a moment to admire the change in the landscape.

Everything had been brown when she walked in. Now it was covered with a pretty blanket of white snow.

If it were light out, the entire woods would be covered in a blanket of snow, which would be beautiful.

Maybe tomorrow she'd see it.

For now, she felt her way back through the kitchen and touched the box of matches that she found earlier. Her phone still sat by the chair she'd napped in, but she didn't feel the need to grab it.

Setting the wood down, she took a small handful of kindling and arranged it in the stove by feel.

After she thought she had it pretty well set, she lit a match just to check and make sure.

It didn't look like very much, and she decided to go out for more. Another thump on the porch indicated that Griff had dropped another armful of wood down.

Maybe she should have gone out and helped him. But she felt ridiculous in the dress.

She'd looked around, even though checking in his drawers felt like snooping, and she did find a flannel shirt that she put on over her fluffy pink dress.

She'd only found one pair of pants, and they were way too big for her. She would wear them if he didn't want to, but she couldn't take his last pair.

Therefore, she sat in the chair and didn't go out.

If she was going to be stuck in this dress for the next who knew how long, since Griff had said he couldn't ride anywhere in the snow on his bike, she didn't really want to be dirty, and she definitely didn't want to be wet.

Regardless, she pushed to her feet, went out, got some more kindling, and brought it back in. She hadn't had occasion to make too many fires in her lifetime, but growing up, she'd watched her parents do it more than once.

She tried to remember exactly how her dad had fixed it up, and she wasn't too disappointed when she lit the kindling and while it didn't catch beautifully at first, it slowly started to burn, and she felt gratified that maybe she was going to get the fire going after all.

Ten minutes later, it was going pretty well, and she was congratulating herself when she heard the door open.

She turned, and Griff walked in.

He had an armful of wood in one hand and carried another piece in his other.

"You got the fire going." He stated the obvious, but he sounded surprised.

"I started working on it after you dumped the first load on the porch. It's been a while, but I remembered a little."

"You made a fire before?"

She nodded and didn't say anything else. She didn't typically talk about her childhood.

"I have to say I'm impressed. I think you've got a better fire going than I would have had."

His words made her glow inside, but she avoided looking at him while she pushed up off the floor where she knelt in front of the stove.

"I wanted to have something ready for you to eat, but there was no way to cook it."

"I'm sorry. I should have come in and made a fire right away."

"It's okay. I found your flannels, and I'm not too cold."

"It's chilly in here. I'm sorry, I guess I had a lot of things I was thinking about and it never even occurred to me that it would be cold in the house and I should get you warmed up right away. I'll try not to be so inconsiderate from now on." He looked truly distressed.

"I promise, I've been fine. I mean, I haven't been keeping warm by chopping wood, and I was a little bit tempted to go out. But my dress isn't exactly suited for it and... I didn't even think about it, but I don't have shoes either."

Her low heels were hardly appropriate for her to be tramping around the woods in.

"I'm sorry. I should've stopped and dropped you off at your house. This was a bad idea."

"Are you regretting that because of my attire? Or are you regretting it because now you realize you're going to have to spend the evening with me?" She tried to make it so that there was teasing in her voice, but she was a little bit afraid that he was having buyer's remorse.

"No!" he said quickly. "I'm actually looking forward to talking to you. We...work together a lot, but everything we talk about is usually diner or food related. We don't have to talk about work at all today if we don't want to."

"Or tomorrow. I assume we're going to be stuck through at least tomorrow?" She tried not to sound like she was dreading it. She actually wasn't. She...wouldn't mind getting to know Griff a little better. They worked together, and she hadn't really considered that he had a life outside of the diner. That he had a cabin.

"Did you build this yourself?"

He grinned. "I had help from a buddy, but yeah. We made everything. Except of course the sink and that type of thing. Did you figure out the pump?"

"I've used that kind of pump before." She wanted to stop talking about that. Continuing on without taking a break, she said, "I haven't had occasion to use it because I couldn't cook anything."

"All right. I have a lamp here somewhere," he said, opening up the cupboard door above the refrigerator. It had been too high for her, and she hadn't been overly curious about what was in the cupboards anyway. She assumed it was the normal plates and that type of thing.

But he pulled out a lamp, holding it carefully so he didn't spill the oil that was inside.

"I never even thought about looking for a lamp."

"I don't use it during the summer. It's usually light enough to see, and if I happen to get up before daylight or stay up after dark, I just feel my way around."

"Well, that makes sense. I feel kind of dumb now. I could have had a lamp glowing at the very least." As she spoke, he walked over to where he kept the box of matches and lit the lamp.

"I figured you probably have enough on your mind. I don't mind either, I like cooking."

"I suppose you need to." She stood awkwardly while he moved around the kitchen, familiar and easy.

"Did you have this recipe sitting on top because it's the one you wanted?"

"I liked it earlier today, and that variation sounded good. I figured I could make it." She wished she would have tried harder. She could have gone out and gotten a few pieces of wood to start a fire at least. Now she felt worthless as he came in from chopping wood and had to cook his own supper. While she...didn't do anything.

"Do you want to help?" he asked.

"It would give me something to do and make me feel a little less worthless." She couldn't hide her relief.

"I'm not trying to make you feel worthless. I just didn't want you to feel like you had to come here and do a lot of work."

"Sometimes we're happier if we're busy."

He nodded, like he knew exactly what she was talking about.

They worked together, her cooking the chicken while he chopped and cooked the onion and gathered the rest of the ingredients.

In no time, they had a nice soup for themselves ready to set on the table. She had set it with the simple bowls and silverware she got from the cupboard, and he had filled up glasses with water from the pump.

"I guess I didn't thank you for coming to get me," she said as he set the pot on the table.

"I wish I would have found out what I did today, earlier."

"How did you find out?" she asked as she sat down in a chair.

He pulled out his chair and sat down as well. "I don't know if you've seen this kid around town. Teenage boy. He used to hang out with Becky."

"Becky that Luke and Kristin are adopting?"

"Yes. He's slowly changed, wearing black and that type of thing."

"I actually did notice that."

"James is his dad."

"Oh my goodness." She was horrified.

Not only did James have a child, but the child was someone she knew around town. That felt more icky than she could imagine.

"I can hardly believe I got taken in by him. I feel so stupid."

"Don't feel stupid. You saw the woman he was with tonight. She was taken in by him too. You're no more stupid than she is."

She hadn't thought about that, but it was true. She had admired that woman, thought she looked suave and sophisticated, but that woman was just as stupid as what Chi was.

Or just as susceptible to someone's lies.

"I don't think I'll ever trust a man again," she muttered.

"I guess I can't really blame you for that, but I don't think that's fair." He didn't give her a chance to reply but said, "I'll pray."

She bowed her head and listened to him say grace over their meal. James never had. She realized that now. Although she hadn't noticed it at the time. She'd been so starstruck and eager to catch his eye that his character had never crossed her mind.

It was easy to see now that she had been looking at the wrong things.

"Amen," she said as Griff finished his prayer.

"This smells really good. It's something I've been thinking about adding to the menu at the diner. Folks seemed to like it today."

"I agree. It's one of those things that I think will be a huge crowd-pleaser and perfect for winter."

He grinned. Like he liked her enthusiasm.

"Except you," she murmured, picking up the thread of the conversation that she had been talking about before they prayed.

"Except me?" His brows furrowed as he dished out a spoonful of chowder into her bowl.

"I will never trust men again, except for you. You... You have been nothing but kind to me, and I'm sorry that I haven't appreciated it."

"We're all like that. We get stuck on ourselves, we forget to look at the people around us. I've been like that too."

"But not with me."

He didn't look at her, but he murmured, "No. Not with you."

That made her wonder what exactly made him notice her and be so kind to her. Did he feel bad for her? After all, starting a diner in the dinky little town of Strawberry Sands wasn't exactly a get-rich-quick scheme. It was more likely the path to bankruptcy.

"Why did you stop at the diner that day?"

"It was the Lord," he answered without hesitation.

"God told you to stop?" she asked, a spoonful on her chowder in midair as she waited for his answer.

"Not in an audible voice. But have you ever had those things that happen and you just realize that the timing was perfect and it can only be God? That's what that was."

"Getting hired as a line cook at a dinky diner in a tiny town in the middle of nowhere was God?" She always thought God worked in bigger ways than that. Richer ways. More lucrative ways.

"Yeah. That is exactly what I mean."

Chapter 10

"Luke, are you awake?"

Luke stirred in his bed, tugging his wife closer and trying to grab hold of the dream that he had been having.

She was warm and soft, and his dream had been sweet and nice. He didn't want to climb out of sleep.

"Luke?"

The last of his dream bubble popped, taking with it everything but the feeling that it left. Nice. He ran a hand down his wife's thigh, her skin soft and warm. If he had to wake up, he could think of a few things he'd like to do.

"Luke? Are you awake?"

Kristin's hand came down on his, stopping it on her thigh She threaded their fingers together but squeezed, like she was trying to get his attention.

She had it. Maybe not where she wanted it, but she did have it.

"Luke?"

"Yeah?" he said, sleep roughening his voice. He was slowly starting to realize that she'd been trying to get his attention for a while.

"Are you awake?" she asked again.

He smiled. "No?"

She rolled, first to her back, then to her side facing him, where her hand came up and touched the stubble on his cheek while her other hand tucked under his thigh.

"What about now?" she asked.

"I'm awake. And ready for whatever it is you have planned."

"Good. I feel like there's something wrong. And I need you to go check."

That was not what he was hoping she had planned.

"Let me requalify. I'm ready for anything you have planned that doesn't get me out of bed."

"Luke! I think there's something wrong."

"Can you be more specific?" he said, hearing the note of concern in her voice and trying to be just as concerned as she was. After all, she was his wife, her concern should be his. But really, he didn't want her to have any concerns, so he would happily deal with whatever it was she was concerned about. She wouldn't have woken him up for just anything. She never had before.

"I don't know. I just have a feeling. Something's off. I don't know what it is, but I can't sleep, and I know there's something wrong."

"Interesting." He sniffed. He didn't smell smoke.

"Is the house on fire?" she asked, and an edge of panic crept into her voice mingling with the concern.

"I don't smell anything. What exactly do you think is wrong?" He was fully awake now, although his body still didn't want to move. He held her a little closer to him, tucking her head underneath his chin while he listened intently. He didn't hear anything. Didn't smell anything.

"I don't know. I just have this feeling. I've had it for an hour now, and I can't shake it. I don't know what's wrong, but something is."

"Is it safe for me to get up and check, or should you do it?"

"Luke!" She slapped at his chest, then slipped her hand behind his neck, and lifted her cheek to press hers against his.

He nuzzled her neck. "Do you think whatever's wrong can wait for a little while? I can think of a few things I'd like to do before I get up."

"How about we put them on hold and do those things after you come back."

"Promise?"

"You know I do."

He smiled. He didn't have to talk her into anything. Oftentimes, it was her talking him into them. "All right. But if anything happens to me, just know that I wanted to do everything before I got up. Not after."

"It's not you. It's something else. I don't know what."

"Did you hear Bruno bark?"

"No. I didn't hear anything."

Bruno was their dog, and he always slept with their youngest daughter, Rita. The adoption of the girls had been final just the week before. Expedited through the state because of someone his mother knew who was in a position to make it go through.

Both of the girls had seemed to be fine with the adoption. They still fought with each other, and his older daughter, Becky, was a little jealous of Rita's dog, Bruno.

Still, they settled in as well as he could expect them to.

"Do you think it's the girls?" he asked as he rolled over and put his feet on the floor, running a hand down his face before he tried to remember where he put his pants.

"It might be." Kristin spoke like she was thinking about it.

"Could it be the old ladies?"

"Maybe. I... I don't think so. But I guess it could be."

Her grandma had started treatments for cancer, and the treatments had been coming along just fine. The doctors thought a few more months of them and she might be in remission, since the cancer had been responding well.

Because of her age, they had been giving her the lowest dose they possibly could. They had to find a balance between quality of life and extending her life. That's what they'd said anyway.

Maybe her gram had some kind of reaction to the treatment that she'd just taken that day.

He found his pants and shoved one foot in at a time, trying to think of what he should do. Check on the girls first? The old ladies?

"You think I can just open the ladies' doors and check in on them? I can't just stick my head in their room." He didn't want to knock on their door and wake them up if there was no problem, either.

"Maybe I should get up too?"

"If we're going to check the rooms, you probably should."

He could stick his head in the girls' rooms, but even that felt a little bit awkward. Becky was a teenager, and he wouldn't go into her room without knocking. Not while she was awake.

He felt a lot better when he heard the sheets rustle and saw Kristin's shadowy form rise from the bed.

He stuck his arms into his T-shirt and padded to the door on bare feet.

By the time he had it open, Kristin had her hand on his back, sliding it around his waist and peeking over his shoulder.

"You ready?"

"Yeah. I'll follow you."

He smiled; sometimes being the man wasn't any fun.

But he didn't want anything to happen to Kristin, so whatever was causing her bad feeling, he would face it first.

"Do you have your phone?" he asked, realizing he hadn't put his in his pocket.

"I do."

"All right, if anything happens, you run, then call 911, okay?" He didn't want her trying to fight anything and get hurt.

"Okay."

Thankful she didn't argue with him, he didn't want to waste any more time convincing her to do what he wanted her to. After all, she woke him up to do his job, it would be kind of silly for her to have him doing his job and then argue with him about how he should do it.

He appreciated that she didn't.

"I'm gonna check the girls first."

"All right."

She kept a hand on his back, and he appreciated that, then he knew where she was as they walked out of the room and down the hall.

Kristin's house was huge, and with all the ladies and two children, they weren't even using all the bedrooms.

It was the perfect house to have as an assisted living center, or if they ever wanted to be foster parents for more children, it would work for that as well.

Luke wasn't sure how Kristin felt about it, but as much of a trial as Becky and Rita could be at times, especially when they were fighting and unreasonable, and even worse when they didn't respond to his logic, he loved them. His life was better because of them, and the idea that there were more children out there who didn't have families who loved them tugged at his heartstrings. He'd adopt more in a heartbeat, and he'd foster them even faster.

Maybe he should talk to Kristin about that.

A board creaked under his foot as he crept down the hall. He wasn't exactly trying to be sneaky, but he didn't want to wake the entire house. It wasn't that he didn't think that Kristin's feeling was legitimate. But it just might be something that they didn't need to check on until morning. Or definitely might not be something that needed to wake the entire house.

With a hand on Rita's door, he twisted the knob slowly and pushed in.

Bruno lay in bed beside the little hump that was Rita's body. She was curled all around him. He lifted his head as Luke opened the door.

"It's okay, buddy," Luke said softly, not wanting the dog to bark.

The almost full moon shone in through the windows, illuminating the room and making it easy to see Rita's hair sprayed out on the pillow.

She was such a sweetheart, and Luke felt his heart swell. He wanted to protect her, give her everything he could, and help her become a productive adult.

"She's too sweet," Kristin said from behind his shoulder.

"She looks like a little angel lying there," he said, looking for just another minute before he closed the door without a sound and slowly released the doorknob so it hooked in the slot.

Becky wasn't quite as much of an angel. She was a little bit more headstrong, a lot more independent, and hadn't submitted to their authority quite as easily.

But he could tell she was trying. She wanted to be a good daughter, wanted to be a help, wanted to actually have a family, especially for Rita's sake. She'd just been on her own for so long, had trusted and been betrayed, had loved and not been loved in return. It had scarred her.

They reached her door, and Luke twisted the knob.

This time, with the moonlight streaming in, it was obvious there was no child in the bed.

"I think this is the problem," he said, and his voice didn't give any indication of the fear that had rooted in his stomach and spilled up through his chest.

He'd caught her walking outside after midnight once already, and she promised him that she wouldn't leave again.

"She promised," Kristin said, agony in her voice.

"I know."

Actually, that wasn't entirely accurate.

"Well, she didn't exactly promise. She told me that she couldn't promise until the next week, and then I never cornered her after that and made her promise."

"That's right," Kristin said.

"But it's been four months. I haven't heard a thing. Surely we would know if she'd been sneaking out regularly."

"I haven't heard anything either."

"I've checked several times at night. And for the first month after they moved in, I was up at four o'clock every morning. She was always in bed."

Maybe he shouldn't have stopped. Maybe she was listening for him to not be checking up on her anymore. Maybe she was just waiting.

He didn't know.

"There's no point in both of us not getting any sleep for the rest of the night. Do you want to go back to bed, and I'll go out and sit on the porch and wait for her to come back home?"

"What are you going to do when you catch her?"

"I guess I'll ask her where she was. We'll see if she'll tell me. I... I don't know what else to do."

"Me, either. If I think of anything, I'll let you know." She paused for a moment, then her arms went around him. "Do you mind if I sit with you? I don't think I can go back to sleep right now."

"I'd love it if you'd be with me. Everything's always more fun when you're beside me." That was the truth. It was a bit of a surprise to him to find that as much of a loner as what he was, he loved having Kristin with him whatever he was doing. He wouldn't have thought that. He would have thought that he needed time alone, but he enjoyed being with her far more than what he expected.

Marriage was definitely the best decision he'd ever made.

He took his wife's hand, and they walked down the steps together.

Chapter 11

The heat from the woodstove made Chi sleepy.

They'd finished supper, and Griff had warmed water for washing the dishes up on the woodstove. She helped with the cleanup, and they put the leftovers in a covered container on the porch.

Then he'd heated water for her to have a sponge bath. There was no tub or any kind of container big enough to put water in for an actual bath.

He'd gone outside, saying he needed to walk around and check on things, while she sponged down quickly and emptied her dirty water.

She was dressed in the spare pants and flannel shirt when he came back in. He had socks that she could wear as well, and a spare pair of boots, although they were way too large.

She didn't mind the oversized clothes. In fact, they were extremely comfortable and far better than the frilly pink dress which was thrown over the single chair in the bedroom.

She didn't know if she'd have to wear it again, and she didn't want to just let it lie in a heap on the floor. Still, she couldn't imagine going back to that after putting the comfortable clothes on, even if she did have to roll up the pant legs and the arms of the flannel.

Working with Griff as they washed the dishes and put them away and cleaned up the meal and fixed the fire and heated water had been easy and intimate, a little different than working in the diner together.

Sometimes in the morning when they were both there before it opened, they had that easy camaraderie where no words were necessary.

This was different though, because they weren't expecting to have a mad rush of patrons, there was no pressure to get the food just right, and there was just a relaxed atmosphere that made her wish that she could do this forever.

With Griff.

She couldn't imagine doing it with anyone else.

Now, she was sitting on the couch, which was definitely not long enough for Griff to sleep on, while he sat on a chair that he pulled over beside her. His feet were propped up on the small handmade coffee table that sat in front of the couch.

"The woodstove should keep the bedroom decently warm, as long as you leave your door open. That's why I put the woodstove against the wall right beside the door. The flue goes out and up the bedroom, and that, along with the heat that travels in from the stove, usually keeps it nice and warm."

"I won't shut the door. I definitely want to be as warm as possible, although the blanket on the bed looked nice and snuggly."

She hadn't sat down on the bed, and she didn't know how soft it was, but as tired as she felt, she figured she could sleep pretty much anywhere right now.

The only problem was, she really didn't want to get up and go to bed. She liked sitting here with Griff.

Maybe if she started talking to him, they'd stay longer. Although, Griff had never been a very talkative person.

"Why did you stay?"

"That first day?" he asked, and she was surprised that he knew exactly what she meant. She wasn't sure how to phrase it exactly, but she hadn't needed to worry. He got her. The funny thing about it was, he always had. From the very beginning.

"Yeah."

He was quiet for a few minutes, and she wondered if maybe he wasn't going to answer. They hadn't talked about too much personal stuff as they worked together. Griff was always focused on helping the diner out, trying out new recipes, and figuring out what folks would enjoy.

She had always bustled around, cleaning and doing dishes and arranging things and making sure the decorations were as good as she could make them. She loved decorating for the changing seasons and trying to make the restaurant as cozy and inviting as she could.

In hindsight, they worked well together, because they focused on different areas and they had different strengths.

"It was because of you," he finally said, sounding like it had been obvious.

"Me?" She tried to think of what she had done. "I didn't ask you to stay."

"Maybe that's part of the reason I did. You didn't ask. But you obviously needed someone. You didn't have a cook, didn't have a waitress, didn't have anything except yourself."

It was true. She was struggling to do it all, having used most of her meager savings to purchase the building and get her first supplies.

"So you just pitied me?" She figured as much.

"I admired you." He paused, and she thought maybe that was all he was going to say, but she didn't understand. There was nothing about her to admire. She was struggling so hard and didn't have a clue of how to make anything successful. She hadn't realized what she was getting into, even though she worked at a diner for almost ten years. Waitressing, cooking, doing it all.

All except the owning part. Which was a lot different than she expected. A lot harder. There was more red tape, more taxes, more fees the government imposed than she had ever imagined. She thought the diner owners were raking in money, and she didn't realize how much money had to go out for all the things that were necessary to run it.

"There's always been something about you that has pulled at me."

Chi sat stunned. There was something about her that pulled him? Like...an attraction?

She couldn't believe it. He'd never even indicated in any way that he might be attracted to her. But that was what he was saying, wasn't it?

He didn't say anything else but sat staring at the glow from one of the cracks in the stove.

She figured maybe that wasn't something that was very easy to talk about. He certainly had never said anything of the sort before. Maybe it was time for her to be a little bit brave too.

She had to admit the dark made it easier.

"So you're attracted to me?" As much as she tried to say that with confidence, it came out more like a question, and a tentative one at that.

He didn't move, his feet propped up on the coffee table, his eyes on the stove. Finally, he grunted and said, "Is that so hard to believe?"

It was. It was extremely difficult to believe. She hadn't looked at Griff as anything other than a hired man. Well, he'd become a lot more than that. And she realized she'd taken him for granted. She hadn't appreciated what he'd done. He'd gone out of his way over and over again to help her. To make her life easier. To do everything he could to make the diner successful. He worked as long and hard as she did, even though it wasn't even his. She hadn't given him nearly enough credit for that.

"Yeah. I guess it is."

She didn't say anything else. She...hadn't realized how much she depended on Griff or how comfortable she felt with him. She couldn't think of anyone else she felt more comfortable with.

But that wasn't attraction.

Although, the idea of kissing him didn't turn her stomach. In fact, she kind of liked it. But that wasn't attraction, either.

Attraction was the hot-and-cold feeling she felt when she was with James. The anxiety, the angst, the desire to have his eyes and attention on her and her only. That was how she wanted to feel.

Although, she felt a little possessive of Griff too.

"Do you remember early this spring when we had that woman in the diner who saw you through the window and walked back to the kitchen?" she asked, thinking about it as she spoke.

"You came in and practically grabbed her by her hair and dragged her out. It is one of my best memories." One side of his mouth kicked up, and she realized that she found him handsome. She'd never thought of that before.

"I did not drag her by her hair."

"I could tell you wanted to. And that makes for a better story."

"I'm not denying that I wanted to. She was..."

"Brassy?" he supplied for her.

She thought about the woman. She'd been exactly the kind of woman that she would have thought would be on Griff's arm. She had a good many piercings, a couple of cute tattoos, and one snake that wrapped up her arm. Her hair was two different colors, a pretty blue and a garnish pink. It didn't quite look like cotton candy, because the pink was too much.

Her hair was brittle, like it had been dyed a lot.

"I thought she was a user," she said quietly. There had been scars from needles on her arms.

"Maybe she had cancer," Griff said easily, presenting the other side without judging her for leaping to a conclusion that might not have been accurate.

"Maybe." She had been skinny enough to be a cancer survivor or someone going through treatments.

"But I think you're probably right," Griff said, his voice still casual.

"Now why would that kind of woman want to break into the diner kitchen and be with you?"

"Good question."

"She's the kind of woman I can see you with." She might as well be honest. She didn't mean to insult him by it, but that was what she thought of when she thought of Griff.

"I suppose at one time it would've been the kind of woman I would've been with. I can see how you would think that."

It wasn't that her past was pearly white. It wasn't.

"I think once upon a time you mentioned that you had grown up with the Amish. Did I hear that right?"

He must have been listening pretty closely if he heard her say that. She didn't admit that to just anyone. She might have been talking to one of her close girlfriends, maybe Kristin or Jubilee.

"My parents left the Amish sect. But they still did a lot of things the same way the Amish did them."

"So you're Amish but not Amish."

"I'm not Amish at all."

Her dad had left her mom after they had six kids, and her mom had married a man who wasn't Amish.

"My stepdad abused us. All six of us kids. I was in the middle, so I didn't get anything any worse or any less than anyone else, but it wasn't a pleasant environment."

To say the least. She left home as soon as she turned eighteen, without even finishing high school. She couldn't stand it anymore.

"So you left as soon as you could," Griff surmised, although she hadn't said.

"Exactly."

"Do you have a high school diploma?" His words were easy, like he didn't judge her whether she had one or not. If she had to guess, she'd say he didn't have one either. He looked like his background was probably very similar to hers.

"No. The day I turned eighteen, I moved out and got a job in a diner. I moved in with one of my sisters for a while, but I didn't want to have the same lifestyle that we grew up in. And that's the direction she was going." She paused. "I went that way for a while."

She'd done things she was very ashamed of. Things she wished she could take back. But life didn't give a person do-overs. It just provided opportunities for them to make different decisions, which, she knew from experience, was very hard.

"It's a wonder you don't hate religion."

"It is. My parents were very religious, but they didn't have a relationship with Jesus. It was all about rules, which is basically what the Amish do in their religion. It's all about following rules, not about loving the Savior."

"The thing that Amish do well is their sense of community with each other."

"They do that very well. And when you're not a part of it, you definitely feel left out. I guess that's what I got from the Amish community, the feeling of being left out."

"You probably had cousins and aunts and uncles and grandparents that you didn't get to see much."

"And when I did get to see them, they talked in Pennsylvania Dutch, which I didn't know, and having people you're playing with have their own secret language that you don't understand makes you the odd man out every time."

"Ouch. Especially when they're your relatives."

"Yeah. A lot of people think that if the Amish leave their sect, they're shunned. But they're not. If they haven't joined the church, they can make the choice to leave. Of course, they're under a lot of pressure to stay. But who would want to?"

"I guess I can see a lot of benefits from a simple way of life."

"It's simple, but it's constant hard work. There's just as much stress involved in being Amish and trying to earn enough money to pay your bills and as Amish move in and the land values go up, their property taxes often increase to the point where they are the largest and most onerous expense they have, not to mention the work is more dangerous and harder and longer and the comforts are fewer." She couldn't imagine going back to that lifestyle. "One night without electricity is more than enough for me."

"It might be two nights. I doubt I'm going to get my bike out tomorrow."

"All right. Two nights, but that's my limit." She tried to inject a little levity in her tone, but the subject matter really didn't allow her to. It brought up memories she'd really rather not have.

"So you worked in a diner? Is that why you ended up buying one?"

"Yeah. I lived with my sister for a while, did the things that she did, and then I pulled away. Of course, when you do something like that, you're no longer accepted, and while she didn't kick me out, living with her became...uncomfortable. I moved in with a friend."

A male friend, but she didn't say that to him. She wouldn't do it now, but she'd done it then, just to survive.

"It took me a while to get out of that lifestyle. It's always tempting to go back. Alcohol does numb your problems for a while. But it is addicting, and it also eats up all of your paycheck, and I was sick of living hand-to-mouth, never having enough money to pay for anything, and always being looked down on by people because I was poor and worked a dead-end menial job."

"You sure people looked down on you? Was it just your imagination?"

"It might've been." She considered that. After all, she didn't go around judging people, not normally. She hardly thought people wasted a whole lot of time judging her. But the thought was there. "Maybe it was just me judging myself. Finding myself lacking. I still do that."

"God doesn't think you lack anything. He loves you."

That should sound odd coming from Griff, but it sounded like something he would say.

"So you were taught that growing up? It's a lot easier to believe from childhood up, I think."

"No. I wasn't Amish, but my childhood is similar to yours. Strict parents that thought religion was more important than relationships, and I rebelled. I rebelled younger than you did and ran away from home when I was fifteen. I probably was in everything you were, even worse stuff."

"So how'd you get out?" She had figured as much. Figured he was into all the bad things.

"I had a preacher take interest in me. I wasn't interested in religion, but he got me off the street, helped me get cleaned up, and showed me that relationships were more important than religion. I... I pretty much hit rock bottom, and I didn't really have anywhere else to go but up. He helped me get my high school diploma, and I ended up in community college at the same time, and I found out that I wasn't as stupid as what I thought I was."

"So you got a degree?"

"A couple of them. I practiced law for a while."

She gasped. "You are a lawyer?"

"Shh. It's not something I'm proud of. I think you'll find that there is a huge similarity to religious people who think religion is more important than relationships, and people on the other side who think they know everything and look down on everyone who aren't as enlightened as what they are. At least I saw a lot of similarities, and I didn't want to be that, any more than I wanted to be religious without a relationship."

"So you left?" He had to. He'd been working as a line cook in her diner for years. He certainly wasn't practicing law. He didn't have time.

"I did. I made a lot of money, because I was determined to be successful. Determined to not fall back down in the pit that I'd come from. But you don't get any more satisfied with a lot of money than you do with a lot of religion."

"I see," she said, although she wasn't sure she believed it. Money seemed like it would solve a lot of her problems. It would give her the prestige she craved.

"Having men look up to you like you're something special doesn't mean anything. It's just a bunch of dust admiring more dust. It's the Creator we should want to admire. It's the Creator that we should want to have a relationship with. It's the Creator that we live for. He owns everything. Money doesn't matter; it's all God's."

Now she saw what he meant. That if she was just getting money so other people could admire her, their admiration didn't mean anything. Or at least it shouldn't. Because they weren't anything but more of the creation.

"I never heard anything like that before," she murmured, still thinking.

"I guess I thought about it a lot while I was working my way up the ladder, thinking that I should be more satisfied than what I was. I just wasn't. I mean, don't get me wrong. It's nice to make enough money to have your bills paid, but beyond a certain threshold, where you're living comfortably, it doesn't really mean anything. It definitely doesn't give you more satisfaction or more contentment."

"So you gave it all up?" she asked.

"Kind of. I walked away from it. I... I guess I was looking for something else, and I happened on the diner and you, and that seemed to be just exactly what I needed."

"So you had just left your job when you met me?" She had never suspected that he was a high-powered lawyer.

"I'd been gone for a couple of weeks. Just drove around on my bike. I went south first, but there's just something about the lakes that call to me. Lake Michigan is my favorite. I suppose, when I was sitting in my office in Chicago overlooking the water, I spent a lot of time staring at it in contemplation."

"It grows on you. There's definitely something about it that calls to me as well." She couldn't believe he was a lawyer. Here she was, didn't even have a high school diploma, and he was working for her. And not only working for her, she'd been taking advantage of him. Treating him like... Not like he was less than, or like he didn't really matter. But like he was replaceable, when she realized now that he wasn't.

"I don't like to mention that I used to be a lawyer. It...changes the way people think about me. I don't want them to think that there's something special about me, or different, or better. I'm just dust the way they are."

"I guess I agree. It definitely changes what I've been thinking. But for a while now, I felt like I needed to apologize to you."

"Apologize?" He sounded truly baffled.

"Yeah. I... You've been a good friend. And I have not. I realized that on the ride up here, I guess. You've always done whatever you could to help me. And I just kind of assumed that you were going to be there. I never thought about how you might feel or even acted like it was important that you stay. I'm sorry."

He didn't say anything for a while, and she wondered if maybe he was angry at her and trying to figure out how to tell her that her apology wasn't enough.

But he couldn't be angry. He hadn't been anyway.

"I guess I never thought that you were taking advantage of me. I just wanted to help you. I... I enjoy working with you, enjoy the challenge of trying to make the diner profitable. I love challenges. And this was a good one."

She didn't see the diner as a challenge. She saw it as work. A stepping stone to get what she wanted.

"The diner serves people, gives them smiles, it provides a place in the Strawberry Sands community for people to gather, to eat good food, and to fellowship with each other. I don't think you understand the place the diner has in the community. It's fun to be a part of that. It's fun to try to make it grow."

That was the most insight she had into Griff's character and why he had done what he had done.

It sounded like it was all about service to him. About serving others and making them happy. About making the diner successful for her, yes, but also about providing value to the community.

He had a real heart for people. One that she admired and respected. One that she could learn from. Because her heart had been very selfish.

"You make me feel really bad about myself."

"How so?" he said, sounding surprised.

"I feel selfish. For me, this has been all about me, and what it can do for me, and how I can benefit from it. I didn't hesitate to shut it down when I thought I found something better. For you, you see the diner as a way to help others. That's...such a great way to look at it."

"That's not all I saw it as." He sounded like he was confessing. And it made her curious.

"What else?"

Chapter 12

Griff sat by the fire, the heat from the stove making him drowsy. Well, at least he had been drowsy before he started talking to Chi. He'd confessed that he was attracted to her, but she hadn't returned the sentiment. He supposed he knew she wasn't going to, but it had made him feel bad. Discouraged. Like there wasn't any hope for them. All she was ever going to see him as was as an employee. Maybe her best employee, but also her only one.

Maybe that was why he told her that he had been a lawyer. That he had worked hard and had been successful. He wanted her to see him as someone worthwhile. Even as he told her that he had quit being a lawyer because he didn't want people to see him that way.

Talk about irony.

And now she wanted to know why else he was working at the diner. He told her the altruistic reasons, and they were true. The diner was a blessing to the people in Strawberry Sands, and he was a part of that on a daily basis. He brought tourists in, just with his strawberry dishes, and with their signature dishes, they'd enticed people as well. This summer, they'd had more repeat visitors than they had the summer before. People who would come back saying they thought of the food of the diner all year and couldn't wait to return to Strawberry Sands to vacation, yes, but also to visit the diner.

That had been his goal. To expand their customer base and have repeat customers.

It seemed to him that that was one way to grow business. A slow way, sure, but a tried-and-true way as well. As long as they continued to have quality food that enticed people to return.

"You don't have to tell me if you don't want to," Chi said, breaking into his thoughts.

He would rather think about the diner, about enticing people to come, than he would try to figure out what he could say to Chi to answer her question.

"I told you. There's something about you that calls me. I... I wanted to be with you. So I stayed."

That was the bottom line. It was all about Chi. He could have helped build a diner anywhere. It didn't have to be in Strawberry Sands.

Strawberry Sands was where Chi was, and so that's where he wanted to be too. He didn't want to be where she wasn't.

"That's the second time you've insinuated that you...feel something for me."

"And I asked you before, is that so hard to believe?" He wanted to be defiant about it, not humble. Being humble meant that he would give her the ability to hurt him. If he were defiant, he kept his walls up. And she couldn't get in.

He was going back to his teenage days, when it was important to protect himself and the people around him. But he could trust Chi. Even if she didn't return his feelings, she wasn't going to make fun of him. She wasn't going to hurt him. She wasn't going to use his feelings against him. She wasn't going to be unkind in any way.

He could trust her. With his heart, with his feelings, with his hopes.

The problem was, he knew she didn't return any of those things, and he didn't want to make her uncomfortable.

Okay, that was a lie. He didn't want to be embarrassed. That was the problem.

"I told you it was. I can't really believe that," she said, and it sounded like she was smiling.

All right. Humor might make it a little easier.

"I liked that you knew it was going to be hard, and you were putting the work in anyway. You were trying with everything you had, putting your very heart and soul into it. I admire that. I admire the fact that you wanted to do everything honestly, that you didn't try to cut corners or get ahead by being dishonest. I admire your grit and your determination. I love the fact that when you come into the diner in the morning, you might be sleepy, you might be a little disheveled, but you're smiling. Not too many people can smile at that hour in the morning, and I love that you can. And at eight o'clock at night when we finally turn the closed sign over, you're still smiling. That means a lot. I admire that, and yeah, I find it attractive."

There. It wasn't as hard as what he thought it was going to be. Once the words started coming, they came pretty easily.

"Wow. You painted a picture of me that I don't really see."

"I see it. There wasn't anything there that I made up. It's you."

"I just don't see myself that way."

"You just saw yourself through my eyes. A little bit anyway." He didn't tell her how he admired the way she supported her friends, how she held babies so couples could eat without the kids crying through the whole meal, even though she was overworked and could barely keep up with the things that she needed to keep up with. How she took a discount for senior citizens, when she really couldn't afford it. All the things that she did that were just simple kindnesses but involved a sacrifice from her. He admired her willingness to sacrifice. That was what it boiled down to.

Chapter 13

Kristin sat on the porch swing, a blanket tucked around her and Luke's arm holding her close.

They'd been sitting there for over an hour. She was freezing. Part of her wanted to call the police and report Becky missing, and part of her wanted to just wait and see if she came back.

"Maybe we should wait until daylight. If she's not back by then, we need to call the cops." Luke's voice cut into her thoughts.

"I was just thinking the same thing. If we call the police, we're going to open up a huge can of worms that we might not be able to get the lid back on."

"I was thinking the same thing. We might lose the girls."

"I mean, the adoption is final and everything, but...it scares me."

"Me too. Plus, I've always heard that you can't file a missing person report for twenty-four hours. I don't know if it's true or not, but I think there's some wisdom in just waiting and seeing."

"Me too. It's just... I feel like we need to do something." They fell silent again, although Kristin was tempted to ask him what time it was.

The last time she'd asked, it had been three fifty.

Snow fell around them, and normally she would enjoy the soft fall of the snowflakes, the hush of falling snow and a town that slept under a winter blanket of white stuff.

She loved the snow. Although she was always ready for spring and summer, snow was just as much a part of her life as summer waves and reading by the beach.

More time ticked by, and Kristin found herself nodding off until a sound by the gate made her pick her head up.

Luke's arm tightened around her in warning, and she didn't say anything. Straining to see through the darkness and the falling snow, she finally saw a small figure hurrying up the sidewalk.

Becky was on the porch before Luke spoke, causing her to startle and jerk toward them.

"Becky. I thought you weren't doing this anymore."

"Really? This is the first time that I've been out since you caught me. I can't believe you're sitting here waiting on me. Did you hear me leave?"

"Where did you go?" Luke asked, ignoring her questions.

Kristin wanted to rush to her, wrap her arms around her, and hold her with relief that she was safe.

Luke didn't tell her she couldn't, and she couldn't see any reason why it would be a bad thing to let Becky know that she was loved and missed.

Getting up, Kristin hurried over. "I was so worried. I couldn't sleep. I am the reason we got up. I just felt like there was something wrong, and when we checked your room, you weren't there. Why didn't you tell us?"

"Were you going to let me go?"

"Where did you go?" Kristin said, holding her close, squeezing extra tight in relief and gratitude that she was safe and okay.

"I can't tell you."

"Then no. We couldn't let you go. You know that."

"We want to be able to go to bed and not have to worry about whether our kids are going to be there in the morning or not. I don't know where you were, but it's snowing. You could've gotten lost. You could've died in the cold weather."

"He walked me home."

"Who did?"

Becky bit her lip.

"How about we sit down on the porch swing and chat for a little while. Maybe whoever it was needs help?"

Kristin was always surprised at how insightful Luke could be sometimes. She also knew he absolutely adored Becky and wanted to believe the best of her. She could just see his brain working to tell him that Becky was only going out to help someone. Or because someone needed her.

Kristin hoped he was right.

They settled on the swing, with Becky under the blanket between them.

"I'd really like a promise from you that you won't do it again. I want that almost as badly as I want to know where you were."

Luke was being as honest as he could be, and Kristin appreciated his realness. Letting Becky know that they were worried and that she wasn't in trouble, he just wanted to know. So he could help her and protect her.

"I have a friend. He helped me when I didn't have a home. After I ran away. He helped me get a job."

Kristin almost made an audible sound, but she bit it back just in time. There had been a boy with Becky when she had gotten hired at Davis and Kim's boarding stable. Back when their baby was born and in the NICU for such a long time.

Of course that was probably the boy she was seeing.

"How old is he?" Luke asked right away.

"That's just it. That's why I can't tell you. He's afraid he'll get in trouble. Because he's old."

"An adult?"

"He's a senior in high school this year."

That was a good bit older. And no wonder he didn't want people to know about them. If there had been anything inappropriate going on, that kid could be in a lot of trouble.

"If he's not doing anything wrong, he won't be in trouble," Luke said, and there was an edge to his voice that wasn't there before. Kristin figured he was upset with this boy who was taking advantage of his little girl.

"He hasn't been doing anything inappropriate at all. But he understands that people might not believe him. Or me. People don't usually believe me," Becky said, sounding a little put out by the whole idea that she could say things and people didn't understand.

"Can you tell us? And if he hasn't done anything wrong, then you won't be in trouble."

Said like that, it seemed like the most reasonable thing to do was for Becky to tell them.

Kristin didn't know how Luke did it, but she appreciated it, because Becky started talking.

"He caught me when I was outside his house, hoping to get in so I could steal some food. He let me in, fed me, and after that, he left the door in his room unlocked so I could get in and out whenever I wanted to. I didn't have a place to sleep at night, so I'd go to his house and sleep."

"With him?" Luke said low, and it sounded a little threatening.

"I slept on top of the covers, he slept under them. But he'd leave a blanket on the chair so that I would be warm. He... He was like a big brother to me."

"A big brother?" Luke said, and there was hope in his voice.

"He always wanted to make sure he took care of me. And I would get out before the sun came up so that no one ever caught us, because he'd been so nice to me and I didn't want him to get in trouble."

"So what's the problem now?" Kristin asked.

"I never told him that I wasn't going to come anymore. After Luke caught me the first time coming back, I had told him that I might be adopted or that I might have found a place for Rita and I to be together. But I told him I'd come back and let him know. I couldn't just not keep my word. But I didn't want to leave again, because I knew that it would upset you and Luke if I left without asking. But I couldn't ask because I knew you would say no."

"Yeah. That's probably true." Luke sighed. "But we could have driven you to his house."

"His parents don't know, and that's part of the problem. He found out his dad was cheating on his mom, and he's been going downhill ever since. I see him sometimes at school, but he won't talk to me. So I thought I would try to catch him at his house and see what was going on, but he didn't want to talk."

"But he walked you home?" Luke asked.

"Yeah. He didn't want me to be stranded in the snow."

Well, that gave him brownie points anyway. Kristin thought she knew who the kid was. She thought that Griff from the diner had been meeting him along the beach. The kid had been slowly sinking down, traveling with the wrong crowd and wearing black, and looking more and more like someone who was working for the devil. The idea of her sweet little girl being around someone like that...

But she was obviously very fond of him.

"Maybe I can see if I can do something with him," Luke said slowly.

"I think he just feels really hurt about what happened with his dad. He wasn't that close to his parents, but at least they were together and he felt like they were honest people with integrity. His dad cheating just messed everything up."

They were quiet for a bit. Kristin was eager to get Becky put to bed so she could talk to Luke. Surely he had some ideas of what they could do. Obviously, Becky couldn't help him, but maybe they could. Or maybe they could help Griff, who seemed to have a rapport with him.

"I told him I wasn't going to be over anymore. He was happy for me that I have a family. He's that kind of person. He wants to see good things happen to me. He understood. But... I'm worried about him."

"Kristin and I will talk about things we can do," Luke said. "I'm sure there's some way or maybe multiple ways that we can give him a hand."

"I promise that I won't go out again at night. Not without you guys knowing where I'm going." Becky spoke without them having to prompt her. Kristin wanted to squeeze her and give her a bear hug and rain kisses all over her face, but she didn't figure that Becky would appreciate that, so she refrained.

She didn't know what Luke had in mind, but she was feeling very optimistic about Becky, about their lives together, about being able to help the boy that Becky cared about.

Chapter 14

Griff lay on the sofa, tired. It had been a long night. He hadn't slept much, because the sofa was not only hard, but it wasn't nearly long enough for him, and he hadn't been the slightest bit comfortable. Not to mention, the conversation that he'd had with Chi had been on his mind the whole time.

She hadn't said that she reciprocated any of his feelings, but she had apologized for not treating him very well.

That really wasn't what he wanted, it wasn't even close to what he wanted, but he thought that maybe he would just have to take what he could get and not be greedy for more. He might not ever get what he wanted. But if he loved someone, he was going to treat her the way love dictated and not allow his actions to depend on her feelings.

That just seemed to be the right way to handle everything, although he wasn't sure whether he would be able to do it or not. It was a pretty hard thing to show love again and again to someone who didn't care about you.

The thought had kept him tossing and turning all night, but he must have dozed off, because as he slowly came to consciousness, he could smell...coffee. And he realized he had heard some clanging and banging like Chi might have fed the stove and built up the fire.

How long had it been since someone else had made coffee for him first thing in the morning?

A long time. If ever. The pastor who had helped him get his life turned around hadn't drunk coffee.

Griff hadn't drunk coffee until he became a lawyer and was working eighteen-hour days. At that point in time, all he thought about was becoming rich and successful, and coffee had helped him stay awake and alert and do more in a day than he normally would have been able to.

Now it was an addiction he didn't want to think about stopping.

He shifted, sitting up on the couch and looking over his shoulder.

His movements had caught Chi's eye, and she smiled at him.

"Goodness, you were sound asleep. I went outside and used the outhouse, and you never even stirred."

"I feel like I didn't sleep at all."

"I can imagine. That couch is so lumpy. It's not the slightest bit comfortable, and it's not big enough. But your bed is really nice," she said with a grin. "Thanks for letting me have it. If we're here another night, I suppose we should switch."

"No. If you're here, you get the bed."

He didn't want the bed. Didn't want to think about sleeping in it while she was out on the couch. That would go against everything he believed.

He turned when he heard footsteps and saw that she was bringing him a cup of coffee.

"I know you drink it," she said, smiling and handing it over to him.

"Thanks." He wanted to tell her that it'd been a long time since anyone had taken care of him like that. But it was just a cup of coffee and hardly something to get so sentimental about. She already knew he had feelings for her that she didn't return. He didn't need to embarrass himself further.

To his surprise, she sat down beside him. That's when he looked at her a little closer. It looked like she'd been crying.

"We got almost two feet of snow. It was pretty deep when I went out to the outhouse. You're going to need that coffee."

"I'm gonna need to chop some more wood too. I'm definitely not getting the bike out with that much snow."

"I heard we were getting up to eighteen inches, but we got more than what they were calling for."

"Sorry. I... I thought several times that I should have taken you home instead of bringing you here. I thought you were going to give me a hard time about that."

"No. I'm glad you did. I needed a place where I could be away and come to grips with the bad decisions I've made."

"Don't be so hard on yourself." He hated that she was blaming herself. Was that what the tears were about?

Maybe it was better that the tears were about that than that she was crying over that loser of a lawyer who was cheating on his wife.

"I want to make sure I take responsibility for my actions. It's true that not everything is my fault, but if I take that kind of attitude, then I'm stuck. There's nothing I can do to change anything because nothing that happened to me is a result of anything I did. But if I look at it like it's all my fault, then I can see where I can change things. You know what I mean?"

He nodded. That made perfect sense. And he was glad she saw it that way. He supposed blaming everybody else made a person feel better, like it wasn't their fault, but it was true that it also stuck them in a corner that was impossible to escape because there wasn't anything they could do.

"It's all about perspective."

She looked at her hands in her lap, and he glanced down at his coffee. Steaming and black, just like he liked it. She'd noticed. Of course, he had coffee pretty much every morning at the diner, and sometimes she made it, although not specifically for him. More often it was him making it for her.

"Why were you crying?" He didn't mean to ask, but the words came out, and now he waited for her answer.

She sat with her head down, her fingers twisting in her lap, her posture tense. Finally she sighed.

"I've wasted a lot of my life. That makes me sad. But it also means that I know what I've been doing is not what I want to do with the rest of my life. So, I guess I was mourning the waste, and then I buckled down and thought about the things I wanted to do in order to make sure that the rest of my life isn't the same."

Did that mean she was still leaving the diner? It was selfish of him to not want her to. He drew in a breath.

"I can admire that. Tell me how I can help you."

"You bought the building for the diner. You told me that yesterday. What are you planning on doing with it?"

Hope stirred in his chest. Hope that she was moving forward with him, and her speech about turning over a new leaf was about getting rid of the lawyer.

"I bought it for you. For us. For the people of Strawberry Sands. I assumed we were going to be moving the diner and we would set up shop there. But when you said that you didn't want to do it anymore, that you were leaving, I guess I didn't even think about it, but I don't want it if it's not with you."

That was the honest truth. He'd had no desire to be a diner owner if Chi wasn't with him.

"I don't want you giving me anything I didn't earn."

"You put in just as many hours as I have over the last few years. You certainly have earned the right to be co-owner of a diner with me."

"Co-owners?" she asked, lifting her brows.

"I won't accept anything less."

She jerked her chin up, then looked back down at her hands. "I wasn't even thinking that you were going to offer me that much. I thought maybe you would hire me to manage it."

"I guess I assumed we'd continue to have the same kind of relationship that we had that works so well. Why fix it if it's not broken?"

"You doing the cooking, creating new recipes."

"And you making people feel welcome, caring about them, making the diner's atmosphere feel welcoming and cozy. I guess I can give you a hand with the books if you need me to."

"I suppose you're a little more qualified to do that than I am."

"I don't think either of us is qualified to be accountants, but I suppose between the two of us, we can make it work."

"I don't like it, it's my least favorite part of my job, but I understand in order for me to do what I do, I have to do it."

"A necessary evil," he said.

She nodded, and their eyes caught and held for a moment. His heart kicked up a few notches, and his breath hitched.

The way she looked at him, with admiration and affection, he wanted to eat it up.

He tried to remind himself that she only liked him as a friend, but it was difficult to do.

She looked away first. "Now that you're up, I'll grab the leftovers from outside and start warming them up."

"There's something to be said for having a woman who knows how to start a woodstove and get the cabin warm for me before I have to get up and walk around."

"Well, I'm depending on you to split more wood. So, I guess I need to keep you fed so you can keep me warm."

"That seems like a good deal."

"It works for me."

Chapter 15

"Thanks for coming to get me. I had a hard time wrapping my head around the fact that someone cared about me so much that they would drive the whole way to Chicago to save me from myself basically."

Chi didn't know what else to say. How could she find the words to tell Griff that she enjoyed working with him? That she had a great time for the past two days? That she really didn't want to be dropped off at her house and have him leave her?

They'd spent a lot of time making plans for their new diner. Figuring out how much time it would take to redo the interior of the new building that he purchased. She had insisted on him writing everything down. She didn't want to be the person who took everything and never gave. She'd pay her way.

He had been reluctant to put figures down and even more reluctant to hear her lay out a plan for her to pay him back.

She had some savings of her own, and she insisted that all the numbers be kept track of.

It amazed her that Griff was willing to put all the money into it.

It also surprised her when he walked her to the door of the diner but didn't step in. They had agreed that they would keep the diner closed for one more day. People were getting out and about, but no one expected them to be open after a storm like that.

"Aren't you coming up to your apartment?"

He lived across the hall from her. Both of them had a one-room apartment above the diner.

"Well, that's something else that I did when I purchased the diner."

"What?"

He looked a little ashamed. What in the world could he have done? He didn't trash his apartment, did he? As soon as she thought that, she knew it wasn't possible. Griff would never.

"I bought a house."

"You did?"

She...wasn't super excited about that. She'd kind of gotten used to having him above the diner with her. It was nice to have a neighbor. She didn't mind being alone, enjoyed it most of the time, but it was nice to know that he was right beside her if she ever needed anything. That was selfish. She had determined to herself that she would not be selfish with such a good friend anymore. She would be happy for him when things went well.

"Where is it?"

"It's the house on the bluffs that was for sale. The one just down from the old schoolhouse."

Her mouth was in an "O," but she couldn't get any words to come out. That was a nice house. A very nice house. "Wow. That house must have quite a view."

"Maybe... Maybe you'd come for supper sometime? I'll show it to you."

He sounded so adorably insecure. And Chi had had such an amazing time within the last two days and had...thought about him so much. She was thrilled that maybe a little bit of what they had at the cabin would carry over. He had said he was attracted to her, but he hadn't said anything about wanting a relationship or wanting to do anything about the attraction. It was like he threw it out there but had zero plans of doing anything about it.

She had had a hard time thinking about anything since he'd said that. When she compared him to James, Griff was better in every way. She found herself realizing that she admired him quite a bit. And she definitely liked him. She had spent more than a little time thinking about kissing him.

"I would really like that," she said, realizing she sounded a little breathless.

"All right then. You settle in today, and we're opening the diner first thing tomorrow morning?"

"That's right."

They'd agreed that they'd keep the old diner open through Christmas while they made plans for the new diner, then they'd take the month of January to do all the improvements that needed to be done and plan on opening it by Valentine's Day at the latest.

That seemed like a good plan to her, and Griff had been on board with it too.

"I'll see what I can do about lining subcontractors up. If I get anything in the works, I might text you to meet me there."

"I'll be there," she said. "Oh."

"Yeah?" He stopped and looked at her with a hopeful expression on his face. Like he was expecting her to say something. Or wishing that she would.

"That chicken corn chowder was really good. I hope you're planning on adding that to the menu."

From the expression on his face, that wasn't what he wanted her to say. But he smiled a little at her and nodded. "I'll do that."

"And homemade bread," she said.

"You got it," he said. He gave her a searching look, and she couldn't pull her eyes from his. Then he turned and walked away. She wished he wouldn't. She felt oddly bereft as he left.

Chapter 16

Griff walked down the steps, his heart hammering.

He hadn't seen Chi since he dropped her off at the diner after they'd come home from being stranded together at his cabin.

He'd thought their relationship was progressing, but he'd had a lot of time to allow the doubts in, and now he wasn't sure where they stood.

Would Chi look at him and smile like she'd been doing in the cabin?

Or was she thinking about her lawyer again?

Surely, now that she knew he was married, she wouldn't be going back to him. She'd said as much, but sometimes people changed their minds.

Just because she knew the lawyer was married didn't mean she could turn her emotions off like they were on a switch. He knew that much about people anyway. Even if his emotions weren't that complicated. He liked Chi, had for a long time, and...he supposed if he found out she was secretly married, he would have to get away from her. Because he wouldn't be able to stop liking her that easily.

Surely she was the same. But, she seemed like the lawyer being married was a real turnoff. Maybe she was just using Griff as a rebound relationship.

He wasn't knowledgeable enough about relationships to know whether that was true or not, or what he could do to avoid it. He just knew he wanted to be with her, couldn't stop thinking about her, and couldn't wait to see her this morning. Even if he was nervous.

He'd come in the front door of the diner, locking it behind him, and had gone through the kitchen and into the hall to grab a fresh apron when his eye caught on a face staring at him through the back door window.

It was unexpected, and he almost stumbled, but caught himself in time. In the dark, he couldn't be sure, but it looked like Rodney.

Odd, that he would show up at this time of morning. He quickly went to the door, unlocking it and opening it.

"Rodney? What's the matter?"

Rodney's face was white, and his eyes wide, like someone who had seen a great horror. He didn't answer Griff's question, so Griff opened the door wider.

"Come into the kitchen. It's chilly out." Not nearly as cold as it would get in January and February, but was below freezing anyway. The snow hadn't melted although he'd been out to shovel the walks off, and one of the Landry boys had plowed the parking lot like they normally did.

Rodney had both arms holding his waist tight and walked slowly in, barely seeming to notice Griff strode beside him.

Griff put his hand on his shoulder, but when Rodney just stopped in the middle of the hall, Griff put a hand on his back and pushed him toward the kitchen.

"This way." He reached around Rodney, opening the door and switching on all the lights as he guided the boy into the kitchen.

"Are you okay?" he asked, looking the kid over, trying to see if there was any sign of injury.

He was wearing a rather ratty looking hooded sweatshirt, with no beanie hat, and he just wore slip on shoes. No boots. Snow was caked on the bottom of his pants, and while he should be freezing cold, he wasn't even shivering.

That fact alone made Griff's heart tremble in fear. There was definitely something wrong, although he didn't think it was a physical injury.

"Rodney. I can't help you if you don't talk to me."

Rodney turned eyes toward his, and Griff almost stepped back. The eyes looked vacant, horrified, or something.

"My mom shot my dad; then she shot herself."

Griff gasped.

"Are they both...dead?" He wasn't sure how else to say it, although Rodney didn't seem like he was in any condition to answer questions like that.

Rodney nodded. "I called 911, but I couldn't stay."

Griff wasn't sure how he got out of there. Usually they would keep someone on the phone...they wouldn't let the kid leave.

"When did you call?" he asked, thinking that the kid was going to need some kind of professional counseling service. Certainly Griff wasn't qualified to deal with trauma of this nature.

"Just before I walked out of the house to walk here. So... A couple of hours ago?" Rodney didn't seem like he was too sure of his answer.

Griff pulled a stool over in front of the oven, and then he turned the oven on, just to provide some heat.

"Didn't whoever you talked to on the phone want you to stay?"

"She," Rodney said derisively, showing the first emotion that seemed real. "Like I'm going to stay in my house with my two dead parents. I hung up on her, and walked out." He looked down at his attire. "Got this at a secondhand store last week. I didn't want to look like my parents. I didn't want to end up like them." He snorted. "I definitely don't want to end up like my parents. They would never wear something like this."

It was better than the trench coat that he'd been wearing around town. But Griff didn't say that. He assumed that Rodney had been buying a jacket at a secondhand store because he had hopefully taken Griff's words to heart, and was moving away from his fascination with death, but he didn't want to wear the clothes his parents had provided. Whatever it was, Rodney was rambling, probably a defense mechanism his brain employed to keep him from thinking about the horror he'd seen.

Not that Griff was any expert in that.

"Man, I don't know what to say. But I think you're going to need to talk to someone other than me."

"I don't want to."

"There are people who can help you. They're trained in this kind of thing."

"They're just going to tell me to find the power deep within myself or something. So much crap. There is no power in me." Rodney hung his head. "I don't need human power. I need... Something stronger than I am."

"God."

Rodney lifted his head. "My dad scoffed at that idea, like religion was a crutch or something."

But it wasn't a crutch. God had just made man so that man needed God. When man refused to acknowledge that need, and depend on the Lord, man needed to depend on something else. Whether it was drugs, alcohol, or some other form of pleasure or satisfaction. Griff and Rodney had talked about it, and it seemed Rodney had been listening.

"A lot of people scoff at religion. We don't want to admit we're weak, that we're nothing without the Lord." Griff didn't know what else to say. What did a person say to a kid who had seen what this boy had seen?

Even in his childhood, he'd never seen anything so horrific. He couldn't imagine that Rodney would ever get the picture of his parents out of his head. Wouldn't get the memories of this night out of his head. What in the world could Griff say to help him?

And then the thought came to him. Maybe he didn't need to say anything. Maybe he just needed to be here for him. To allow Rodney to take the lead in letting him know what he needed.

Griff figured when he was a kid, he never heard anything that anyone said when they tried to force it down his throat. It was only when he was actually interested that he paid attention and learned.

Sometimes that was still true. It took maturity, or to be able to take one's focus off of oneself, and to actually listen and hear when someone else was saying. To take an interest in them, even when one wasn't interested. To take time out of a one's life and give it to someone who needed it.

"I got to thinking after you and I talked," Rodney said quietly.

Griff grunted.

"About death, and life, and...I don't know a whole lot about religion. My parents took me to church on Easter and Christmas. I suppose we went a few other times too. But, the way I see it, there are only two sides. The side you're on, and the side I was on."

"There's not going to be a tie at the end," Griff ventured.

Rodney nodded, like he already had thought of that. "I know which side wins in the end."

"That's right," Griff said.

"Why would I fight for the losing side? I can't change the outcome. I can only choose which side I'm going to be on."

"It's your choice. God gives everyone free choice."

"I know. I tried to distance myself from my parents. They're not choosing for me. But, it's kind of hard."

"To a certain extent, what your parents do will be with you all your life. If you have good parents, parents who set a good example for you, who do what's right, who try not to be selfish, who do everything in their power to make your childhood one where you learn how to become the kind of adult who thinks of others, and serves God...that stays with you."

"The other kind of childhood stays with you too. I think so, anyway," Rodney muttered.

"Tonight will never leave you."

"I'd already decided I wasn't going to allow my parents to define me. But this... I can't even process it. My parents are gone. Because of my mom." Rodney sounded like he couldn't believe it. Like he was in shock, and didn't know what to say or do.

Griff didn't know what to say or do either.

Just then the kitchen door swung open, and Chi breezed in.

"Good morn-" She cut off mid sentence as she saw he was not alone in the kitchen.

Somewhere in the back of his mind he processed the fact that she seemed happy and cheerful. Maybe even a little more so than her usual. But the smile froze on her face as she took in the somber atmosphere that lay thick and heavy in the kitchen.

"What happened?" she said, her tone completely changed, concern dripping from every syllable.

Griff waited. This was Rodney's news to share if he wanted to. He looked at the boy. Rodney looked up at him, met his eyes, and jerked his head just a bit, before he looked back down at his hands.

Griff took that as an assent for him to be Rodney's mouth. He couldn't imagine telling a bunch of people what happened, and Rodney had already told it twice.

He didn't want to leave Rodney alone in the kitchen, but he didn't want to talk to Chi in front of him. Finally, he decided it was better to stay with the kid, who was technically not a kid anymore, but had just been through a huge shock and obviously needed someone to lean on.

He lowered his voice, and said, "His mother shot his father, and then herself. Rodney found them."

Chi's eyes opened wide, and she gasped and covered her mouth with her hand.

"That's terrible," she murmured, her eyes filling with compassion and going to Rodney.

Then, understanding dawned in her eyes, as she looked back at Griff. She understood that the man who had just been killed that morning was the liar that she had almost moved in with. He could almost see the questions swirling on her face, but her eyes went back to the boy in front of him. Griff was so proud of her when she pushed whatever she was feeling aside, and focused on him.

She took a step forward, tentatively, as though she wasn't sure. Then, she closed the distance between them and put her arms around Rodney.

To Griff's surprise, her tender touch broke through whatever barriers Rodney had erected, and he lay his head on her shoulder and began to sob.

Chi patted his head like he was a little boy, and murmured reassurances to him.

Everything would be eventually okay, Griff knew. Not for a long, long time. Rodney had a lot of nightmarish days to get through. A lot of things he was going to have to process, and hopefully, this would pull Rodney from whatever edge he'd been on, and draw him closer to the Lord. And eventually, everything would truly be okay.

Griff knew that was the best case scenario. There was also the possibility that it would push him back, away from a God who would allow his mother to kill his father.

Hopefully, the discussions they'd had about free choice, and being responsible for your own decisions would resonate with Rodney, and he would remember that both his mother and his father acted independently of what God wanted and of what Rodney could do with his life. He didn't have to allow them to determine his future.

Of course, he would also have the grief of working through the tragedy of losing both his parents, no matter how upset he was with his father, possibly his mom as well. Losing a person's parents was never easy.

Knowing that the diner would probably become a gathering place for the community, Griff turned to the stove. He already had the oven on. And he needed to be ready to serve comfort food to a shocked and grieving community.

While he did that, he prayed. Surely God could take this tragedy and use it for good. He prayed that God would help guide Rodney in the direction that he needed to go. And not allow this to turn Rodney away.

Maybe it was a little bit selfish, but he hoped that somehow this tragedy would also draw Chi and him together.

Chapter 17

Chi flipped the open sign closed and leaned against the door, not able to contain her sigh of relief. It had been a long, hard day.

James was gone.

She could hardly believe it.

Finding out that he was married had totally killed any feelings she had for him. It was disgusting, the idea of being with another woman's husband. She had zero interest in that. But, still, it was hard to believe that the living breathing person she spent so much time talking to over the last few months was no longer living and breathing.

The last she'd seen him, standing at the gala with another woman in his arms, so alive, so bright and vibrant. Even if he had been a jerk and a liar and a cheater, she hadn't wished death on him.

She couldn't say for sure if she had been his wife that she wouldn't have done the same thing. She hoped not, but emotions were hard things to control, and anger and jealousy and hurt were some of the strongest.

Still, the focus had to be on Rodney at this point. The poor kid. He was just launching into life, and to have this happen would certainly affect everything he did from then on.

Chi had found out during the course of the day that he had been an only child. His immediate family was dead. He was technically an adult, since he was 18, and he hadn't yet graduated from high school. What a start for a kid. He wouldn't be eligible to be fostered. The state would view him as an adult.

His mother had a sister, from whom she was estranged, and his father had been an only child, whose parents were dead.

Rodney, for all intents and purposes, was pretty much alone in the world.

How terrible that must be.

Although, Chi could relate a little. She didn't have the best relationship with her family, although she knew they were still there. Still available if she truly, truly needed them.

"Are you okay?" Griff asked, and she startled. She hadn't heard him leave the kitchen and approach her.

He put an arm on her shoulder, and she wanted to lean into him. To put her head on his chest and just allow him to hold her. To hold him. To feel the comfort of another human, and think about something other than tragedy and sorrow.

"How is he?" she asked, looking up at Griff instead. Rodney had gone back to the kitchen, refusing all offers of counseling, answering the questions the police had asked, even taking a ride to the station. But they brought him back.

"I guess he's as good as anyone could expect. He's not laughing, but... He doesn't have that vacant, shellshocked look on his face anymore." Griff seemed truly concerned. And Chi knew it wasn't an act. He'd spent a lot of time talking to Rodney before this had happened, and he seemed to really relate to the kid.

"Are you seriously going to take him home?" Chi asked, knowing that throughout the day different people had said that was what was going to happen. She hadn't really talked to Griff much at all, since he'd been busy in the kitchen and she'd been busy waitressing all day.

"Kind of funny isn't it?" Griff said, seeming thoughtful. "I just bought a house. It was big and empty, and I wondered exactly what I was doing at times. After all, I was pretty happy just living over the diner."

"But if you can afford to live somewhere nicer, why wouldn't you?" she asked. She'd been wondering that for a while. If he was able to afford a place like the one on the bluffs, which was one of the most expensive pieces of property in the area, he certainly hadn't needed to live above the diner for the last few years. It had made her totally reevaluate everything about Griff. But, having the experience that she did with James, where money and prestige just hid a cheating heart, she had to reevaluate how important money and all the things that came with it, was to her.

"No." Griff shook his head. "I was pretty happy with the diner. I only bought the house... I don't know why."

She got the feeling that he actually did know why, he just didn't want to tell her. Or maybe he didn't want to tell anyone, and it wasn't just her. Griff was a private guy.

"I came out to tell you that I was going to head home with him. I'll be here in the morning." He paused, his hand seeming to squeeze her shoulder just a little bit before he dropped it to his side.

"Thanks for letting me know. I can finish up. And, if you need some extra time or whatever tomorrow, I'll muddle my way through."

"I know all you have to do is ask, and there are about twenty people in town who would be more than happy to lend you a hand." He put a hand up. "I know you don't like to ask, but if you need to, you know they're there for you."

She lifted her chin, but didn't say anything. It was hard for her to ask for help. She wanted to prove that she was worthy. That she was capable. Maybe that was why she was so attracted to money and prestige. She didn't want to be the person everyone else had to help. She wanted to be the one helping.

"You know, a lot of people would really appreciate the opportunity to be a blessing to you."

Griff didn't say anything else, he just stared at her for a moment, and then turned around and walked back to the kitchen.

She hadn't considered that. That her needs provided an opportunity for other people to be a blessing.

She thought being needy made her weak. And maybe it did in a way, but a person couldn't be the strong one all time. Maybe it just took a certain amount of strength to admit that a person needed help.

She'd thought money made a person strong, but that wasn't necessarily true.

There were so many things that happened in the last week, she felt like her brain was going to explode from all of her thoughts jumbled around each other.

She finished cleaning the diner, turned out the lights, and instead of going up to her apartment, she let herself out the front door. She needed to take a walk.

Normally she would head down to the beach. Even though it was dark there was just something about the sound of the waves, the feeling of the air coming off the water, the rippling moonlight, and the feel of the sand under her feet. Next to the water the snow would be melted. Although, it might be icy on the rocks.

But she didn't go that way. She turned up the sidewalk, and started walking up the street.

She thought of Lana at the bed-and-breakfast. She seemed so matronly and calm. And wise. It felt like she needed a little wisdom. Maybe that's why her feet turned up.

But it wasn't Lana she met on the sidewalk. Lana's daughter, Sunday, walked down with her hands shoved in her coat pockets, her beanie cap pulled low over her head.

"Hey there," Sunday said as they got closer. "What a day, right?"

Chi nodded. "I'm exhausted, but my brain won't stop. For some reason I was thinking of your mom."

"She went to bed. She has the flu or something. I'm not sure what it is, but she's tired. I put my son to bed, and I'm taking a little walk down the beach, but then I told her I would watch for the last guests to come in."

"Oh. Okay," Chi said, feeling disappointed.

"If you want to walk with me, you can," Sunday offered, as though reading her mind. For some reason, she didn't want to be alone.

"Do you mind?"

"Not at all. I just needed out of the bed-and-breakfast for a little bit. I can't help but think about what happened, and...you know how you always want the best for your kids?"

"I'm sure you do."

"I'm sorry, you don't have children."

"I think if I did, I would agree with you wholeheartedly. Of course you want the best for your kids. We do everything we can to give them everything they need."

"I think I do. But... I don't know. I just...my ex-husband was wealthy. He came from a wealthy family. I thought that meant prestige and I don't know, like money solved all the world's problems. But it doesn't. In some ways, it just makes them worse."

"Really?" Chi had heard that before, but she couldn't say for sure that she agreed with it. After all, in her experience money solved problems.

"Up to a certain point, I think it does. It's true that money doesn't buy happiness. Once your bills are paid, once you have the ability to buy groceries without worrying about whether or not you can afford them, you know, the basic necessities. That's really all you need. Anything after that, doesn't really affect your happiness."

"And you know?" Chi said, thinking that there was probably more to the story.

"A little I guess. After all, it doesn't make you happy in the long run to do things that are wrong."

Chi knew that had to be true. Knew James wasn't going to be happy cheating on his wife forever. That it didn't matter how much money he had, he didn't seem to be happy with anyone. Not his wife, not Chi, not the woman he was with. Nothing satisfied him.

Maybe that's the way she was a little bit.

"You know, I guess I can relate to that some."

"Relate to not being satisfied no matter how much money you have?"

Chi laughed. "I've never had that problem. Having too much money. But I was thinking I could relate to the idea that I always want more. Whatever I have, it's not enough. And I'm not sure why."

"Are you trying to prove something?" Sunday asked, and that seemed like a wise question.

"I think I might be. That… That I'm worth something. Somehow I think money makes that happen. But it doesn't, does it? Being rich doesn't make your character any more valuable than being poor. Money doesn't affect your character."

"And that's what really matters."

"Yeah. Actually, maybe being rich makes it easier to have less character." She wasn't sure about that, but she could kind of see it.

"How so?" Sunday asked, sounding baffled.

"Well, if you have enough money that you don't have to worry about whether or not you're going to have your bills paid, then your attention goes to other things. Like a romantic partner that you're not married to."

"Maybe that's more alluring. Because I can see how if you're not worried about your bills, you have room in your mind for other things. Things that might not even take you away from the Lord, but that are intrinsically wrong. After all, when you don't need God, you have a tendency to not pay any attention to Him at all. But, when you need Him, all of the sudden you're giving up the things that you don't really need, and turning toward Him."

"Yeah. I guess that's what I was saying too."

"But if you're poor, wouldn't you be tempted in other ways?"

They had reached the end of the sidewalk and walked through the deep snow toward the beach while Chi thought about that.

"Maybe you would be tempted to steal? Or cheat your employer or be dishonest? Or lie in order to get money."

"Everything seems to be about money, doesn't it?"

"And it shouldn't be." Chi was sure about that, but her whole life had been about money. About gaining wealth and position. About being looked up to, and what she didn't realize was that being looked up to because she was rich wasn't really something to attain. But being looked up to because she had character was.

She had been chasing after the wrong thing all this time.

"Right. You really shouldn't. Although, as a parent, I want to do the best for my son. I want to give him everything, and I feel like I already failed him because I'm not with his dad. I mean, I don't even know sometimes if he realizes it, you know? We divorced when he was still so young, he doesn't really know any other way. Still, I want the best for him."

That seemed like a very mature thing, to want the best for someone other than oneself.

"If you're doing the best that you can, there really isn't anything else you can do, right?"

"That's just it. Am I? Are there other things that I could be doing? It seems like there is. Like should I be taking him to play groups? Enrolling him in a better preschool? Taking him for more walks along the beach? Am I working too much, too little, am I giving him enough toys, not enough? I just... I wish someone could just say this is what you need to do, and then I would have all the exact information right at my fingertips, and I would know exactly what to strive for."

"Maybe just teaching him to love God, keeping him safe, giving him healthy food, and making sure you spend time laughing together... wouldn't that be enough?"

"Yeah. I guess. I suppose it doesn't really have anything to do with what happened today, other than I feel like Rodney's mom was very selfish. She saw her own pain, and she "fixed" it," Sunday said, using air quotes. "I like to think that even if I were in that kind of pain, actually, I've experienced that very thing, and the thing that kept me from crawling under my bed and staying there, was the knowledge that I needed to take care of my son."

They had made it out to the beach, and stood at the end of the snow line, listening to the waves, and watching the play of moonlight on the water.

A cold breeze blew, and Chi shivered, but she didn't want to turn away. She liked talking. Sunday had some wisdom, and she was hoping to straighten out the confusion in her own head.

She thought more and more that she was falling for Griff, but she worried a little that now that she knew he had money, that it changed the way she thought about him.

That seemed selfish, selfish in a different way than Rodney's mother had been, but selfish all the same.

"Selfishness seems to be like something we all fight."

"I think so. I want to sleep rather than get up in the morning and take care of my kid. I'm annoyed that he has to get up so early. I want to give my ex a hard time because he's happy with someone else. It makes me mad that he could be happy without me. What did she have that I don't?"

"That's so hard." Chi had thought about that a little bit when she had seen James with the woman on his arm. Although Chi had been sure that the woman had money and power and position, which made her better than Chi. But, the lack of character had been all James. And again, that was what really mattered.

"Yeah. I'm sorry. I'm mostly over it. Other than wishing I had done better for my child."

Chi thought about the difference between Sunday, who obviously loved her child and wanted the best for her, and Rodney's mother, who hadn't been thinking of anyone but herself. Of course, the deep grief, the heartache, the pain of having her husband be unfaithful, it had to be horrid. But... Hadn't she given a thought to what her son was going to do?

She would never know. Maybe there was something in the woman's head that had made her think she was doing the best thing for her child, but Chi didn't want to be deceived like that.

"I guess it's just important to follow what the Bible says. God gave us his Word for our handbook, and as long as we're following that, we'll be raising our children right. Maybe there are lots of different ways that work. Maybe like there's lots of different foods that are good for us. But, there are foods that are bad, and we can tell that. And the way we tell whether we're doing the right thing by our child, is whether or not it lines up with the Bible, with what the Bible tells us to do."

"That's a good thought. I guess... I guess if I have two choices, obviously, choosing the one that lines up with Scripture, is the right choice. If neither one of them go against Scripture, then maybe... Maybe it's up to me and my preferences."

"I think that's a reasonable assumption. If God wanted us to know it, it would be in His Word."

"Sometimes I wish He would have spelled everything out, instead of giving us principles, and expecting us to use our brain to think about them."

Chi laughed. "I have to agree about that."

She had known for sure that she did not want to have anything to do with a married man. It hadn't even been that hard to leave James and not look back.

The harder thing was trying to figure out what to do about Griff. She liked him. Quite a lot. And she thought it was just because of who he was. Not because of what he had.

"I better get back."

"Me too. It's cold."

"It's hard to believe it was almost eighty degrees less than a week ago."

"I know. At that time, it was hard to believe that Christmas was coming. Now, Christmas seems a lot more believable than eighty degrees.

They laughed together as they walked back up the sidewalk. Chi hadn't figured anything out, nothing more than Griff was a good man, and she admired him because of that, not because of what he had.

But she really couldn't expect him to believe that. After all, she'd been drawn to James, and it was obvious to her now that what she liked was what he had, not who he was.

She parted ways with Sunday at the diner, with Chi going around back, a little sad because Griff was no longer upstairs with her. Maybe it was selfish thinking, and she didn't even realize it. Turning the thought around, she said a short prayer, thanking God Griff had been there for Rodney, and Rodney wasn't alone.

Funny, after she was done, she was smiling, not because she was happy for Rodney exactly, but because it felt good to be happy for other people. She supposed that was part of taking the focus off of oneself and thinking about others. She stopped seeing her own problems, when she put her focus on others.

Maybe she was more selfish than she realized.

Determined to do better, not just in that area, but in so many other areas, because she would have said that she was pretty much okay, but it was funny how just in the past week she'd seen how much she needed to grow.

Maybe Griff deserved someone better than she. Someone with as much character as what he had.

The thought made her sad, and she turned her thoughts toward the next day, and tried to think who she could ask to help her in the diner. Tried to think that it was an opportunity for someone to be a blessing to her, rather than her being an imposition to someone. And she had Griff to thank for that mindset change.

Chapter 18

"Can I talk to you for a minute?"

Becky walked into the living room where Kristin sat with Luke. The older ladies had gone to bed, and Kristin thought Becky and her sister were in bed as well.

"You can," Luke said, giving Kristin a look.

Kristin could read that easily. He was curious and concerned. Becky was not dressed in her nightclothes. She had street clothes on and she carried her coat.

"I promised you that I wouldn't sneak out of the house anymore."

"And as far as I know you've kept that promise. That goes a long way toward helping us to trust you in the future." Luke spoke easily, but his hand moved from the book he had been reading to Kristin's. He threaded their fingers together and squeezed.

She liked that sign that they were a team.

"So I'm asking you now if I can go out for a bit."

"Can you tell us what you're going to do?" Kristin asked.

Becky bit her lip. She hung her head for a moment, not in discouragement, but almost as though she were considering whether she should tell them or whether she shouldn't.

"I heard about what happened."

"You mean about Rodney?" Luke said gently.

Becky nodded.

"I think that has made us all sad. Are you okay?" Kristin asked gently, wondering if this had somehow brought back memories of her parents, or if it triggered something, maybe something that was familiar to her. Kristin's heart broke at the difficult childhood Becky had.

"I'm fine. But… Rodney helped me when nobody else did. Not that nobody else wouldn't, he just… He helped me when I asked him. And… I'd like to be there for him."

Kristin and Luke exchanged a glance. Kristin wasn't sure whether this was something to do with romance, or whether it was just a friend wanting to be there for her friends. That's what friends were. They were there in the hard times. They came, just to sit and be supportive. To be a body when someone needed it. They didn't need an invitation, and they didn't allow someone they love to be alone in a hard time.

Kristin loved that Becky was that kind of friend. It didn't surprise her. Becky was fiercely loyal. But, Rodney was eighteen. Old enough to be an adult, but young enough to be a love interest. It made her a little bit uncomfortable.

"I think it's fine if you go see him. From what I heard he's staying with Griff, but he'd be at the diner right now."

"Chi told me he's working after school there, from the time he gets there until closing."

Luke nodded at Kristin's words.

"And I think you're old enough to walk to the diner by yourself." Luke gave Becky a long searching look. "And as long as you sit inside the diner and talk to him, that's fine."

Becky nodded.

Kristin figured she understood what Luke was saying. It wasn't okay for her to sneak around to see him.

Luke glanced at his watch. "It's eight thirty. They're probably just finishing up at the diner. I think in normal situations you should be in by nine, but would nine thirty be long enough?" he asked, lifting a brow at Kristin, who nodded immediately.

"That's good. Maybe tomorrow I can talk to him some more if he wants?"

Luke nodded. "I think that would be fine."

"Thank you." Becky turned and shoved her hand in her jacket as she walked toward the door.

Kristin waited until she left before she said, "Do you think they're just friends?"

"I hope so. She's so young. But, she had to grow up fast. And, whatever it is, when something hard happens to someone that you care about, you want to be there for them. I guess I just didn't feel it was right to tell her no."

"So this makes you just as nervous as it makes me?" Kristin asked softly.

Luke nodded. "I don't think Becky is going to lie to us. But I do think she's pretty headstrong. I guess... Maybe if she had been raised in our house we'd handle it a little differently, but I don't think you can treat kids like they fit into a cookie-cutter."

"I think you're right. Different situations and personalities require different parenting techniques."

Luke squeezed her hand, and then his fingers slid away from hers as he put his arm around her and she leaned her head on his shoulder. Neither one of them knew what they were doing. All they could do was pray that they were making the right decisions and that they could guide Becky into an adulthood where she loved God and served him. That was her goal.

Chapter 19

Becky put her hand on the door, and looked in the diner. The Closed sign hung facing out, but there were still lights on and she could see Rodney mopping the floor.

She'd seen him at the funeral, which had been two days ago, and she'd seen him once before that but hadn't gotten a chance to talk to him very much.

She hated that she hadn't been able to be around for him, but she had seen that he seemed to be forging a relationship with Griff, who seemed like he was a good man. At least Luke said so, and she trusted Luke.

Biting her lip, she knocked on the door.

The sound made Rodney's head jerked up, and he squinted, like he couldn't quite see into the darkness beyond the door.

She pressed her face against the glass.

His eyes widened, then his lips curved up in a little smile as he hurried to the door.

At least he wasn't scowling.

He wasn't wearing black anymore either. She'd been a little worried about him. Finding out that his dad wasn't perfect had been a hard blow. Surely losing both parents the way he had had been another hard blow, although she felt like he looked better now than he had before.

"Beck Pet!" he said, looking pleased to see her.

"Dixie." She tried to sound tough and mature, and hide the insecurity that slithered around in her chest, the fear that said he wasn't going to want to talk to her, or see her.

"Hey, kid," he said, putting an arm around her shoulder and squeezing. "It's good to see you."

"I've wanted to see you for a while." She put an arm around his waist and squeezed for a minute, before she backed up. She didn't want Luke and Kristin to have any reason to think that she was doing anything wrong.

"Come on over here and we can sit down for a minute." He waited until she nodded before he called in the general direction of the kitchen. "I have a visitor. I'm going to be talking to her for a minute."

It took about three seconds as they walked to the table, before Griff stuck his head out the doorway of the kitchen and said, "Her?" looking around like he couldn't find the "her" in question. Then his eyes landed on Becky. "Oh. She's one I approve of." He jerked his head at Rodney before he disappeared back in the kitchen.

Becky thought she heard voices and low murmuring, but she forgot about that as she slid into one side of the booth and Rodney slid into the other.

"So how are you doing?" he asked, while she was still trying to find her words.

"I came here to ask you that."

His eyes fell a little, like he'd been pushing the thoughts that he didn't like out of his head, and her words reminded him that he was supposed to be sad.

"I'm doing fine."

"That's what you're supposed to say. What's the truth?" Becky could tell by the look on his face that he really wasn't fine.

Rodney pulled a napkin from the holder, then, almost like he didn't know what to do with it, he set it down on the table, and ran his finger along the edge. Finally he looked up.

"Sometimes there are people that you love because you have to. You know? Like your parents. They're your parents, so you automatically have to love them." He paused for a moment. "I figured out over the last few months that I love them, but I didn't really like them all that much. Especially my dad. I didn't realize there could be a difference between people that you love and people that you like, but there is."

Becky had never considered that either. She loved her sister, but she didn't always like her. But she liked her sometimes.

But she really liked Luke and Kristin. *Really* liked them. They were good people. The kind of people that she wanted to grow up to be like. She didn't want to be like her parents. There was a part of her that was slowly beginning to understand that in order for her to grow up to be like them, she had to listen to them, and take their advice. Because they were trying to get her to grow up to be something different than what she had been born into.

She didn't always like that. She wanted to do what felt good. But, what felt good didn't necessarily lead her to become the person that she wanted to be. Maybe she was a little young to learn that lesson. Because no one else at school seemed to understand that. But, maybe that gave her a leg up, figuring that out early.

It's what Rodney seemed to be saying. Maybe not exactly, but close.

"I like Griff. I like him a lot. He's... He's the kind of man I want to be." He shoved the napkin away and leaned back in his seat. "I didn't like my dad. And I don't want to be like him. But, I'm not happy that he's gone. And I feel a little guilty because I don't like him more."

"I don't think you need to feel guilty."

"The pastor that I've been talking to the last week or so said the same thing. He said that sometimes God puts trials in our lives to push us toward Him. But, sometimes we let those trials draw us away from Him. That's what the devil wants. I've never seen it so clearly, but there are two sides."

Becky nodded. She figured the two sides thing out a long time ago, but she thought about the trials. She wanted to have a home, and was a little angry at God for making her different than everyone else. But, being different than everyone else meant that she understood things that other kids her age didn't. God had given her that too. And she could kind of see how the things she'd gone through could make her stronger and better.

And how Rodney losing his parents could make him stronger and better too. If he let it.

"I thought you didn't like pastors."

"I like Griff. And he's the one who suggested I talk to the pastor. He wanted me to go to counseling, but my mom spent years in counseling, and look what happened to her."

Becky nodded. She wasn't convinced counseling did much for anyone either. Maybe it just depended on the quality of a person's counselor. But how did she know whether she was getting a good one?

"But Griff highly respected the pastor, and he told me as long as the pastor gave me advice that followed the Bible, I should take it."

Becky nodded, tucking that away. She wasn't sure about that. Wasn't the Bible just an old book?

"Has the pastor helped you?" Becky asked, just wanting to make sure Rodney was doing okay. He looked sad, but he didn't seem... Lost or depressed. In fact, it was almost like the death of his parents had pushed him toward Griff and that had ended up being a good thing for him.

"I think so. Probably the best thing he showed me is that for every decision we make, there are consequences. He used the whole sowing and reaping thing, but I don't do much farming. Still, it's not hard to understand that when you decide to cheat on your wife, you're not going to only hurt yourself. You're hurting a lot of other people. So you want to make sure that the decisions that you make are good ones. Not just for yourself, but for the people around you."

Becky nodded. The decisions her parents had made had hurt her and Rita a lot. That wasn't hard to see. And she already had decided she wanted to be different. But, Rodney was saying that meant she had to make different decisions. The problem was, she didn't know which decisions to make differently. She supposed that's why she needed Kristin and Luke.

"It's not just the big decisions though." Rodney said, thoughtfully. "Everything. Whether I decide to sit around and watch TV, or whether I decide to work today. That's going to affect the person I become. It seems like a stupid thing. A little thing. What was a little TV going to hurt? Or what's a little fun with friends going to matter? But everything builds over the years of a lifetime. And I want to do things that build a strong foundation and a good life. Not things that pull me away from the Lord and tempt me to do bad things."

He seemed like he wanted to say more, but he closed his mouth and just looked at his hands.

That was something else Becky needed to think about, because she never considered that before either.

But she glanced at the clock on the wall and saw that she really needed to go.

"I promised I'd be home by nine thirty, and I wanted to be early. They...I think they'll let me talk to you every day if that's okay with you?" She never could quite figure out where they were at. She liked him, and wanted to be friends with him, but he was a lot older than she was and he might think that she was just a little kid who he didn't want to spend any time around. But, if he wanted to spend time with her, she would. She owed him a lot. Maybe he didn't save her exactly, but he got her the job at the horse farm with Davis, and her life had changed for the better since that point.

"I'd like that. I can take a break any time, so when you show up, I'll just let Griff know that I'm on break. We could talk for half an hour or so."

"I'll tell Luke and Kristin. I know they'll let me come over for that long."

They smiled at each other, and Becky thought it was a friendly smile. Maybe Rodney didn't think she was just a little bratty kid who was more annoying than anything.

"Thanks for all the things you did for me," she said, as she slid out of the booth. She didn't want to get all mushy. She wanted to be tough. But, she really did owe Rodney more than a thank you.

"Anyone would have done it."

She shook her head. That wasn't true.

"Take care of yourself, Dixie."

"Don't steal food out of anyone's house, Beck Pet."

She stuck her tongue out at him, then wished she wouldn't have because it was a childish thing to do. But then she laughed when he stuck his out at her.

She turned, feeling the warm heavy feeling that person gets when they spend time with someone who knows they're not perfect and likes them anyway and walked out of the diner.

Chapter 20

"I think he's doing pretty well," Chi said to Griff as she dried her hands on a towel and then carefully hung it on a hook. Things had slowed down since it was just before closing time. The two weeks since Rodney's parents' funeral had gone by quickly.

Rodney was out sitting at the table with Becky, taking their half an hour talk like they'd done since Becky had come to see him more than a week ago.

"I agree," Griff said. He hung the frying pan that he'd just cleaned on the hook above the counter and turned and leaned against it, crossing his arms over his chest.

Chi wasn't sure exactly where their relationship was. It was almost as though he was waiting for her to make some kind of move, but she wasn't sure what that was.

She also thought that maybe he was waiting to give her time to get over whatever issues she might have with James's death, or maybe their breakup, or whatever. But, she realized that her feelings for him weren't really that deep.

Not the way her feelings for Griff felt.

"It's pretty amazing the way he's taken to you. And you've done such a good job with him." She wanted to say more. But she didn't know how to word it. To tell him how she admired how he'd stepped into the role model position, how he'd gently guided Rodney without forcing him, how he had understood his grief and given Rodney room to be sad, while gently guiding him in the direction he should go.

Griff shrugged a shoulder.

"And he's talking to Pastor because of you, too."

"That's just the Lord using this to get a hold of Rodney's heart. I think maybe he was going in the wrong direction, but this all seemed to turn him around."

"I'll not argue with you. It probably is the Lord, but you allowed God to use you."

"You too." His eyes met hers, and she didn't flinch from it.

She supposed he was right in a way. Rodney knew she'd had no idea that his dad was married. And she'd taken every opportunity she could to let Rodney know Griff was a good man.

"You know Rodney and I have been looking at draft horses online."

Chi nodded her head. It is something they'd all been doing anytime there was time at the diner that they had a little bit of downtime.

"Rodney seems quite taken with them."

"Strawberry Sands seems to be a horse friendly beach, and I thought maybe I should jump into it too."

Chi's eyes widened. "You're thinking about getting horses?"

"Drafts. Percherons, actually." Griff reached around and pulled his phone out of his pocket. "I found this guy, Cord Stryker, in North Dakota. He raises draft horses, and makes sleighs. I thought it would be kind of fun to have draft horse sleigh rides to go along with the beach rides that the town offers in the summer."

"Oh my goodness. That's brilliant!" Chi exclaimed.

"We pretty much have Rodney to thank for it. It was mostly his idea." Griff swiped on his phone. "It might not takeoff. It might just be something to keep the locals entertained during the winter, but Rodney seems really interested in it, and I thought that I have the means to encourage it, and it might be something... We could do together." He lifted his eyes and met hers again, and Chi felt like maybe he was including her in that too.

"Here." He handed her his phone.

"These are gorgeous!" Chi said, as she looked at the photo of a man with several small children around him, holding onto a big, docile-looking horse. A small woman who looked like she was expecting, held onto its partner. The horses towered over them, but even from the picture, Chi could tell from their eyes that they were sweet and gentle.

"They're beautiful," she breathed.

"That's kind of my reaction too. And Rodney has been pretty interested."

"I think it's brilliant to give him something to keep his mind off of the things that have happened to him, and give him something constructive to do. And it would give you something to do to bond."

"You always joined our discussions when we talked about the drafts. I... I thought you might be interested too." Griff was so adorable, sounding a little insecure, but looking so tough and strong with his arms crossed over his chest, his bald head shining in the light, his muscles bulging and his boots planted in a wide stance on the floor.

Chi lost her train of thought as she looked at him.

"I'd really like to know what you're thinking right now," Griff murmured.

Which of course made her cheeks heat as she yanked her mind back from thinking about how good Griff looked, and tried to remember what they had been talking about.

"I don't think you do," She said, with a nervous laugh.

His arms dropped, and he took a step forward. "I assure you, I do." He touched her shoulder, and she forgot how to breathe. "I like that look."

"I like how you look," she said, her eyes fixed on his chin, because she couldn't quite look him in the eyes as she said that.

He grinned, a grin that showed her words made him happy.

"Are you trying to tell me that you're not interested in the horses?"

"No," she breathed, trying to pick up the train of that conversation and formulate her thoughts into words. "I just... I just... Like you. A lot."

She hadn't gotten her mind to focus on the horses. But Griff didn't seem to mind.

His smile got bigger. "I like you too. I guess that's why I want to spend time with you. That's why I want to know if you're interested in the draft horses too."

"I'm interested."

Not just in the draft horses.

Maybe she should tell him that.

She took a breath. "In you. And in the horses."

"Seems like I might come with a kid."

"I love Rodney too. And he's not exactly a kid."

"I think he's someone who's going to need some help for a while though."

"Maybe he needs a mom and dad."

"That's what I was thinking." His hand came up and brushed her cheek, and she leaned into it. But then his face grew serious.

"I told myself I would give you time to get over James."

"I'm over him. That was a shallow, stupid infatuation, where I was more interested in his money and position than I was in the man himself. That's not the way I feel about you."

"Hmm. How do you feel about me?" His thumb brushed along her chin and the edge of her jaw, and she put a hand on his side to steady herself.

"Like you're the kind of man a girl could fall in love with."

"I didn't think I'd ever hear you say something like that to me."

"I mean it. I... I'm definitely falling in love with you."

"It's about time. I've been in love with you forever. I think since the first day when I parked my bike in front of your diner and saw you trying to do everything yourself. I felt that was a girl a guy could get behind."

"Beside. We'll be beside each other."

"Beside. I like that a lot better."

He bent his head and trailed his lips along her temple. She closed her eyes and shivered, moving the hand that had been on his waist to steady her around just because she wanted to be closer.

He moved his lips along her jaw before they settled on her mouth.

Later she thought it was appropriate that they had their first kiss in the diner kitchen. They'd spent so much time there together. So much time because it had taken her forever to figure out that Griff was the kind of man a girl could grow old beside.

He lifted his head. "So are you going to go with us to Cord Stryker's farm in North Dakota to see the Percherons?"

"Next week is Christmas." That seemed to be the only thing her brain could latch onto. Kissing Griff was dangerous to her mental stability.

"I thought we'd go the day after. We're closing the diner down, and we're going to do the renovations. It will take a day to drive out and a day to drive back. If we like the horses, I'll buy them, and he'll bring them in sometime when the weather cooperates."

"Yes," she said, smiling up at him. He could ask her to go to the moon with him, and she would have said yes. It didn't seem to matter where he wanted to go, she was ready. Maybe that was because she trusted him.

Funny, after James cheating on her, and cheating on his wife, and cheating on everyone, she should have had a bigger problem with that. But Griff was just the kind of man who was dependable. Who was there. Who would help her. He would help Rodney, he would help whoever needed him. And he would stand beside her. She could bank on it.

"While you're in the mood to say yes," Griff grinned. Chi held her breath. "I... I'm not asking you to marry me, but I'm telling you that's what I want."

It took her a minute to process that. But she thought she understood. He was letting her know that he wasn't playing games.

"I know you're not the kind of man James was."

"Thanks. I didn't want you to think that I was just messing around with you. I wasn't sure what you were thinking after what happened with James."

"I'm thinking James was a jerk. And he was a lot different than you. I knew that then. That you were different. I just didn't understand that it was because you had character and he didn't. I do now." She touched her lips to the side of his neck. "And whenever you're ready to ask, I'm ready to say yes."

"I don't want to rush you into anything."

"I guess you're a better person than I am, because I do kind of want to rush you into something." She smiled against his skin, and he drew his fingers lightly down her back.

"Then maybe we need to talk about a date."

"Can it be before we go out to get the horses?"

He laughed, and pulled away, looking down into her face.

"Are you sure?"

"I'm sure. New year, new diner, new horses, new hobbies, new businesses in Strawberry Sands. Why not a new family too?"

"That's a lot of new stuff."

"Maybe we ought to check with Rodney. He might not want to share you right away."

"Rodney's fine with it." A voice came from the doorway. "In fact, Rodney's kind of relieved that you two are finally talking about this. It's been pretty obvious to everyone in town Griff's had a crush on you for years. And it's that obvious to me that you finally figured out that Griff is quite a catch."

Rodney sauntered into the kitchen, a smirk on his face, but genuine happiness in his eyes.

"All right then. Rodney's good with it, I'm good with it, and sounds like you're good with it too." Griff looked down at Chi. She felt a little bad that he'd known for so much longer than she had, and she figured that there had probably been some pain involved with that. She hated the idea that she hurt someone she cared about so much.

She couldn't change the past, couldn't fix it either. All she could do was apologize and try to do better.

"I'm sorry it took me so long to get smarter."

He laughed a little at that.

"But now that I finally figured things out, figured out the obvious, what everyone else always knew, I'll try hard not to be that dumb again."

"You weren't being dumb. You were just looking at your past and making decisions based on that, and that's normal."

"But fixable," Rodney interjected.

"I think you've learned something from Pastor," Griff said, giving Rodney a playful bump on his shoulder, before grabbing him and pulling him into a sidearm hug, with Chi on one side and Rodney on the other.

"So Chi just said she'd go with us to look at the Percherons at Cord Stryker's place in Sweet Water, North Dakota. Are you still game?"

"You bet," Rodney said, and while he tried to seem chill about it, Chi smiled at the excitement in his tone.

"All right then. It might not be the day after Christmas, because it sounds like I might be having a wedding."

"Really? You have a wedding that fast? Don't you need… Time to plan?"

Griff looked at Chi, but she was already shaking her head. She knew she didn't want all that. She just wanted Griff. "I think we have plenty of time to plan. Just a celebration with our friends here in town, and some good, easy food, and low stress, and just the people who are important to us."

"That sounds good to me," Griff said, and he dropped a kiss on her forehead. She closed her eyes, and couldn't help but be amazed at how quickly her life had changed from what seemed like hopelessness, when she decided to move in with a man she wasn't married to, to total peace and contentment with a different man, one who had character and integrity and who truly cared about her.

It was an amazing feeling, and she knew as long as she was with Griff, she would be with a man who loved his family and would be faithful to his wife.

Epilogue

The whole town had gathered to see the horses unloaded.

January had been a bitterly cold month, but the entire upper Midwest had a massive February thaw, just in time for Valentine's Day.

Sunday tucked Blake's scarf under his chin, and made sure his ears were covered by his beanie cap.

It was warm compared to the frigid temps they'd had all of January, but she still wanted her kid to be dressed for the weather and not get sick.

"Look mom. I can see them," he said, pointing to the trailer where Mr. Stryker led the first dapple gray Percheron off the trailer. Maybe in celebration of Valentine's Day, or maybe just because, the horse's mane was braided with pink and red ribbons. They trailed down its silver white coat, creating a sharp and beautiful contrast.

"So big," Sunday breathed, not meaning to talk out loud.

"It makes Cord, who is not a little guy, look small," Kristin said beside her. She stood with her husband and their two girls between them.

Sunday was happy to have the horses as a distraction. Valentine's Day was a lonely day for anyone who didn't have someone to share it with.

Even when she was married, Valentine's Day hadn't been a happy day. Her husband never wanted to spend it with her. She never really felt loved or valued while she was married, but on a day that was special for couples, to be completely ignored, made her feel even worse. She'd taken to ignoring the day and treating it like any other.

Still, as a single mom, it made her long for things she knew she probably would never have. There weren't a whole lot of men who were interested in a woman who already had a child with someone else and a failed marriage under her belt.

Sunday swallowed and forced a smile on her face as the beautiful horse lifted its head. The wind blew its mane and tail, making it look majestic and beautiful.

"Here comes the other one!" Blake said beside her, his tone hush, but with plenty of excitement in it.

Sure enough, Mrs. Stryker, smiling at the reaction of the crowd, brought the second horse off. It, too, had red and pink ribbons that flowed in its mane and tail, and it was just a hair bigger than the first one as it came to a stop beside it.

They were gorgeous together. Sunday had heard from the rumors around town that Chi and Griff and Rodney had picked out a pair of mares who were in foal. They were both due in the spring, and they were hoping to start their own herd of Percherons, giving buggy rides and sleigh rides in addition to their work at the diner, which they were still moving to its new spot at the edge of town. Everyone thought the horses would be a great addition to the two riding stables that were already there. Strawberry Sands would become known as the horse lovers destination on Lake Michigan. Already they'd had interest, and it was rumored that someone was coming in to build a hotel not far outside of town.

That was all mostly good news for the people in Strawberry Sands.

Sunday was a little bit sad that the small town vibe might get overrun by commercialism, but she was happy that it would be good for the businesses in town and for the people who had grown up there and chosen to stay.

Her mom had mentioned casually that maybe there would be eligible men arriving in town, but Sunday had brushed that off.

She was focused on raising her son, and she really wasn't interested in getting married again. After all, marriage had been a miserable experience, and she didn't want to go down that road again, no matter how lonely she was now.

Shaking those thoughts away, she tried to focus on the happiness of the day and smiled as newlyweds Chi and Griff held hands as they spoke with Mr. and Mrs. Stryker, Rodney standing beside them.

She could feel in her bones that it was a good day in Strawberry Sands. A good day for new beginnings.

JESSIE GUSSMAN

Enjoy this preview of *There I Find Hope,* just for you!

There I Find Hope

Chapter 1

The scent of rotting flowers made Sunday Landry want to puke.

The flowers weren't really rotting, but the smell made her sick nonetheless. For the rest of her life, she would hate the smell of flowers because she would associate it with the funeral of her son.

She wiped her cheek and listened to the lady in front of her as she spoke about growing up in Strawberry Sands and how she had not talked to Sunday since she was a child and how sad she was that Blake had drowned.

Sunday listened. Truly she did. Or at least she tried to. But she didn't really hear anything. It felt like a hundred people screamed inside of her head, arguing, fighting, although she didn't know over what, all she knew was that she could hardly stand it, and she wanted to get away.

Except, one could hardly run out of the funeral of one's son.

Plus, she hadn't quite gotten used to the idea that her son didn't need her anymore. There was the idea in her head that she needed to stay, to take care of him, that he needed her. Responsible mothers didn't just walk out on their kid without taking him with her or making sure he was cared for.

But her son lay stiff and cold in the casket, and it was all her fault.

Why had she decided to go on a walk on the beach?

Why had she stood admiring the horses and allowed her gaze to track off her son for even one second?

It wasn't like she had spent three hours not paying any attention to her son at all.

Blake had known better. He'd grown up around Lake Michigan. He knew he couldn't just run into the water without a life vest and without his mother's permission.

But he'd been chasing a ball. A huge, rogue wave had knocked him down. Sunday had turned around in time to see that.

She called to him immediately, started running right away, but her feet sank into the sand and it felt like she ran in slow motion. That was what her nightmare had been every night since. Running in slow motion.

She kept running and running and couldn't go any faster. Couldn't reach the water in time. And when she did get there, she couldn't find him.

The waves had been high, the riptide strong, and while she knew she would have jumped in the lake to save him, she couldn't see him.

She had her phone out of her pocket dialing 911 as she ran and was mostly incoherent as she spoke on the phone.

They sent people anyway, divers, men with boats, someone even showed up with a dog. An ambulance had sat on the beach, its lights flashing, like there was some hope that they would fish her son out of the water and he would still be alive and they would rush him off to the hospital and he would survive.

Even as she prayed for that to happen, she knew it was impossible. Although God was a God of miracles, wasn't He?

Apparently she didn't qualify for miracles.

She hardly ever asked for anything. She asked for one little thing—the life of her son—and God did not grant her wish. Her desire. Her one longing.

She didn't even ask for her marriage to be reconciled. She hadn't asked for it to be saved. She hadn't even asked God why her husband had cheated, after he'd spent the years they'd been married neglecting her and spending time on his hobbies and online rather than with her.

She just asked for the life of her son.

And God said no.

She supposed she felt the way a child usually felt when they wanted something with all their heart and their parent turned them down.

She felt a little angry, a little put out. Annoyed. Heartbroken. Was there something worse than being heartbroken? If there was, Sunday was that thing that was worse. The very worst thing that anyone could become was what she was right now.

How did one survive, let alone get over, the death of their child?

Why had she walked on the beach that day? Why had she taken her eyes off her kid? Why hadn't she made him hold her hand?

She knew why. She lived here. She'd grown up here. Lake Michigan was something she respected, yes, but not a scary thing. And she thought she'd trained her son to obey. To listen. To respect the lake just as she did.

"You know this is just one of those fluke things that happen. Something you couldn't have stopped. Something you couldn't have changed. It's just God's will."

Really? Was God's will for her to lose her child?

She looked at the lady who was patting her arm. She recognized her as someone she'd grown up with. Gone to church with. Known all of her life. She wanted to grab her by the throat and pin her on the floor and tell her that God didn't will for her son to die.

It was her fault. She was the world's worst mother. She didn't deserve to be a mother. Blake should have had someone better.

She didn't manage to smile, but she nodded and wiped the tear that trickled out of her eye.

She couldn't go back to her apartment above the candy store. There were too many reminders of her son there. His toys, his clothes, a load of his laundry was still in the dryer. Tuesday had been a nice day, and she decided that she and Blake would go for a walk instead.

He begged to take his ball, and she consented without really thinking about it. It would give him something to do as she walked up the beach, thinking about life and things and giving herself a break from the struggle of trying to make her business profitable.

Thankfully her mom paid her for cleaning the rooms at the bed-and-breakfast, or she would have gone under three years ago when she moved to Strawberry Sands after her divorce.

Strawberry Sands was growing, getting bigger every year, more popular with the tourists, and she had high hopes for her candy store.

But now? She never wanted to set foot in her apartment again. Someone else could handle cleaning it out, except she couldn't stand the thought of that either. Couldn't stand the thought of every memory of her son being wiped out. His toys gone. His clothes gone. His presence gone from her life.

She turned back to the well-wishers and tried to focus on their words.

Then, the only thing that could have made her day any worse happened.

Her ex walked in.

Glenn's new wife held tight to his hand while her son from her first marriage held her other hand.

Sunday recognized them easily. She'd seen them multiple times. During and after the divorce.

Apparently Diana ran around with Glenn for a while before Sunday figured it all out. Up until that point, Sunday had been trying to work on her marriage. To get in shape after having a child so her husband would find her attractive. To cook his favorite meals and spend time rubbing his back and feet, asking him questions about his day and listening as he spoke. Sending him sexy texts and buying new lingerie. Reading tons of articles with titles like "what men like in the bedroom," studying them, and putting every idea possible in practice.

Of course, once she found out about Diana, she figured out exactly why Glenn was no longer interested in Sunday.

Diana was everything Sunday wasn't. Slender, with the body of a ballerina, flexible and supple. She was actually an inch or so taller than Glenn, willowy, thin, graceful, and she could probably twist herself into all the pretzels that the articles recommended.

Sunday, on the other hand, still carried around the extra baby weight she had before she even had a baby. She had wide hips from her father's side of the family and no bust.

She was a pear with an apple belly.

Not that any of that mattered now. It wouldn't bring Blake back.

Glenn didn't stop at the back. He moved forward with confidence, walking up the aisle.

She talked to him on the phone, although by the time she was able to call him, there was nothing he could do. And with Glenn being a practical man, analytical and data driven, he didn't bother to make the drive to Strawberry Sands. After all, if Blake was dead, there was nothing for him to come to.

Except the funeral, apparently.

Sunday had sent him the details but hadn't expected him to attend. They'd shared custody, with Glenn seeming to be happy with two weeks with Blake in the summer, and two weeks over Christmas, and an occasional weekend throughout the year.

Probably Diana was happy with that.

Sunday couldn't imagine only seeing her son for four weeks and a few days every year. Her world revolved around her son. Him and the candy shop.

Glenn didn't bother to wait in line; he walked around the folks who were standing, which was pretty much everyone in Strawberry Sands who hadn't already shaken Sunday's hand or hugged her, and he pushed in front of the person who was next without bothering to say "excuse me."

"Mother of the year. Right here," he said.

Yeah, she didn't expect sympathy from him. He wasn't exactly a compassionate person. He was the data analyst for some bigwig company in Chicago, and facts were all that mattered to him.

"Glenn. Everyone says it was an accident. Don't be so hard on her," Diana said beside him, her voice as smooth as chocolate, even if her look was a little condescending. Maybe that was Sunday's imagination, since she had to look up to her. With her tall, willowy figure and her long blonde hair, gorgeous blue eyes, and features that looked like they were lifted directly from an airbrushed magazine, she could have been a model.

Still, any kind of compassion was a lifeline especially after Glenn's few words. He didn't need to say much in order to hurt her already aching heart.

Sunday swallowed. The lessons from her childhood came to the forefront; they'd become automatic over the years, her default. Thankfully.

"I put his favorite outfit on him. He's wearing his favorite sneakers. I know he can't take his toys with him, but I put a few of his favorites in the casket." Her voice, already soft, broke on the last few words.

She turned her head, unable to look directly at the still form of her son but letting her eyes drift to the corner of the coffin. Casket. Casket was a much better word. Coffin sounded so...dead.

She swallowed again. Her throat tight, sore from crying and from trying not to cry, and from being unable to stop crying, maybe from a little screaming as well.

No ever said that when one loses a child, crying takes over one's life. The thought of it, doing it, trying not to do it, recovering from doing it, thinking about doing it again.

It was all there. All in her heart. The crying. Everything.

Glenn lifted his chin, acknowledging her words while at the same time making sure she understood she wasn't on his level. She was beneath him.

The child beside Diana fussed a little, tugging at his mom's hand, holding on it, leaning down.

"Be still," she said, and the words sounded harsh to Sunday.

Sunday wanted to tell her that she needed to be kind. To appreciate the little tug on her arm, the squirming child beside her, not to worry about whether he was inconveniencing her or not, because the day might come when she didn't have to worry about him moving. She didn't have to worry about him wanting to do something other than what he was supposed to do. When he would be gone forever.

"He doesn't have his red truck. That was his favorite." Glenn leaned over the casket and looked at it dispassionately, like the kid that was lying there so still was not his. "Of course, if you were actually a mother who cared about him, you would have known what his favorite color was."

Glenn's words hurt. She already felt like she was a terrible mom, and while she knew that Blake's favorite color was blue, and Glenn obviously didn't have a clue, was just saying things designed to put her down and hurt her, his words just confirmed her thought that she was a terrible mom.

"But being with you all the time, he was turning into a bit of a sissy. Last time he was in my house, he wanted to play with one of Breanna's dolls. I wasn't going to let that happen." Glenn gave a humorless laugh, which Sunday barely heard.

It was one thing for him to insult her. She deserved it. It was another thing for him to say something so unkind about her son.

After she recovered, she would realize that there really wasn't anything that terrible about what he said, but maybe it was the grief, maybe it was her lack of sleep, maybe it was just the fact that she had lost her only child and she was completely devastated, but his words made red fill up her vision until a rage burst in her chest, until the default actions of her childhood were totally obliterated and the only thing she could think of was to hurt the man who had caused so much pain in her son's life.

"You are a—" and a word, profane and vile, came out of her mouth. It was a word she had never said before in her life, but it rolled off her tongue like she'd said it since babyhood, smooth and fitting and so very, very satisfying.

But that wasn't the most amazing thing that happened. At least, hearing the story told later, the most amazing thing was that her fingers curled into claws, her face twisted in outrage, and her body lunged at her ex-husband, knocking Diana and Sidney down in the process.

Pick up your copy of *There I Find Hope* by Jessie Gussman today!

A Gift from Jessie

View this code through your smart phone camera to be taken to a page where you can download a FREE ebook when you sign up to get updates from Jessie Gussman! Find out why people say, "Jessie's is the only newsletter I open and read" and "You make my day brighter. Love, love, love reading your newsletters. I don't know where you find time to write books. You are so busy living life. A true blessing." and "I know from now on that I can't be drinking my morning coffee while reading your newsletter – I laughed so hard I sprayed it out all over the table!"

Claim your free book from Jessie!

www.ingramcontent.com/pod-product-compliance
Lightning Source LLC
LaVergne TN
LVHW012112070526
838202LV00056B/5708